A

LOVER'S

SHAME

THE RAMSEY/TESANO SAGA

I

ALTONYA WASHINGTON

A LOVER'S SHAME
Copyright© 2011 by AlTonya Washington

ISBN: 9780982978146

This is a work of fiction. Characters, names, incidents, organizations and dialogue in this novel are either products of the author's imagination or are used fictitiously.

Printed in USA by CreateSpace

Who else could I dedicate this to? Ramsey fans rule!

FIRST PROLOGUE

August 2004- Monterey California...

"I can always do this next week, you know? Let's go..."

Sabella Tesano's laughter mingled with her moans as her husband's deep, quiet voice vibrated against her chest.

Pike Tesano's voice was pretty much muffled given the fact that his bronzed face was half hidden in the generous swells of his wife's cleavage.

Belle clutched a handful of his clipped dark hair and tried to tug him from his preferred spot inside the V-neckline of her satin tunic. "Stop now, come on." She spoke close to his ear. "You've been planning to take this meeting for weeks."

"Then what's one more day?" Pike's voice was a quiet growl then.

"The hospital board's gonna be too upset if you turn around and cancel at the last minute." She pressed her cheek to his temple. "It's for the kids, remember?" She smiled when his sigh fanned out the bodice of her blouse.

The reminder managed to pull Pike from his 'preferred spot'- just a tad. "Sometimes I really hate being the philanthropist of the Tesano family." He voiced the complaint while nibbling the pulse point at her neck.

"Stop lying." Belle tugged the collar of the shirt he wore beneath an oak sweater and coffee-colored jacket. "The sooner you finish the meeting, the sooner we can get to the lodge."

Sabella's innocent mention of the lodge in Big Bear filled Pike's throat with another low sound. The couple planned a visit whenever a trip to California was on the horizon. The mere mention of the place was enough to intensify the frenzy of Pike's hormones, which had simply been set to simmer.

Belle's laughter filled the rented Infinity once again as Pike resumed his *attentions* toward her bosom.

"Isak…"

"Mmm mmm," he refused and persisted in pressing her back against the passenger door.

"Come on…"

"I'm trying…"

Sabella knew her face would've been beet red were her complexion anything but a rich pecan brown. "We can't get too wild in my mother's driveway, you know?" She bit her upper lip when he lifted his head. Her long almond stare was expectant as she judged his reaction to her warning.

He shrugged. "Windows are tinted." He resumed the act of gnawing the length of her neck. "No one can see us," the soft depth of his voice was an aphrodisiac within itself.

Belle's lashes fluttered and she was fast losing her will to resist her purely irresistible husband. "She'll know it's us…"

"You're gonna surprise her, remember? She won't be expecting you anyway. Now shut up and give me what I want."

"I love you very much." Again, she spoke close to his ear.

The words stopped Pike. He raised his head once more. His expression was set and serious as he cuffed his hand about the base of her neck. "You're everything to me." He said.

It was their usual back and forth wordplay. The simple phrases that meant so much were used whenever they parted ways.

"Alright, alright," Pike muttered, drawing a hand through the blue-black waves of his hair when he moved back to let her up from the seat. "Hope I can focus on this damn meeting," he grumbled rolling his eyes when she tugged the flaring hem of her skirt back across her bared thighs. "Hope you feel good sending me out into the bad world without my nourishment."

"Oh…" Sabella leaned across the gear shift and plied him with a kiss that said more than words ever could. With infinite care and attention, she caressed his tongue with hers, and then broke the contact briefly before beginning the act all over again. The helpless, adorable sounds Pike uttered filled her with surges of triumph and warmth for the love he showered her with.

Again, she broke the kiss, winking devilishly when he fixed her with a hurt expression. She was wiping away faint smudges of her lipstick from his mouth and cheek when he pressed his forehead against hers.

"Go handle your business," she cupped his face and squeezed. "Get back to me quick."

Easing his forehead from hers, Pike nuzzled the top of his head beneath her jaw. "'Kay…" his tone could've been the personification of disappointment. He put distance between them and pointed. "Get outta here before I change my mind."

Belle gathered her things and left him with another wink before moving out of the car.

Pike didn't put the car in drive. Instead, he preferred to watch her go. He settled into the dark, decadent leather seat, relaxing his head against the rest. His charcoal stare; hooded and desire-filled, followed her every move. He dipped his head a bit in order to maintain the view of her long legs bared by the hem of the skirt he'd wanted to take her out of.

Muttering an obscenity then, Pike forced himself to look away. The sight of her sashaying up steps wasn't going to do a thing to ease the stiffness below his waist. With that thought in mind, he floored the gas, enjoying the powerful rev of the engine. He put the car in reverse and set off.

Determined not to make a sound, Belle twisted the key into the top lock on her mother's front door so as not to alert the woman to her presence. Belle never liked going so long without a visit. With everything going on though, it had been difficult to travel to her native West Coast from upstate New York where she now lived with Pike.

Work kept her as busy as her married life. The Ramsey name hadn't given her an open door to the fashion world, not that she'd expected it to. Of course, that meant she had to work even harder for her spot. Thankfully, her talent was masterful and it was slowly yet surely opening those doors for her.

Her husband of four years was just as busy. Pike had been put in place to take over the Tesano family's philanthropic efforts per his grandfather's wishes. It went without saying that the young couple was extremely busy.

And extremely in love. Business trips and fashion events kept them traveling yet offered moments for romantic getaways around the world.

Still, Belle was determined to spend time with her mother. She couldn't wait to get started on a few hours of togetherness. She didn't call out for Carmen, preferring to tip through the airy, beachfront home and find the woman to surprise her. She heard what sounded like voices and followed them toward the kitchen located near the back of the main level.

"I can't!"

"Mama?" Sabella tilted her head in response to the whisper/hiss. She was smiling although a curious frown did begin to tug at her brow.

"It's always been so easy for you to *suggest* I do that, Bri. Try walking in my shoes and give me your opinion then!"

On the other end of the phone line, Briselle Ramsey sighed and silently cursed herself for breaching the conversation with her sister-in-law.

"Honey," Bri began in a soft; and what she hoped, calming tone. "You've walked in those shoes of yours for too long. If you're not careful, that hate's gonna eat you alive."

"Hell Bri, the hate's *already* eaten me alive."

"I don't believe that. You couldn't love that girl the way you do if you were eaten up by hate."

Carmen couldn't respond though it didn't stop her from casting a murderous glare toward the phone where Briselle's voice drifted in through the speaker.

"Carm, I don't mean to sound insensitive about this, it's just… you've lived with all this-this horror for too long… we all have."

Eyes narrowing, Carmen turned to face the phone. "What the hell, Bri? Have you…? God…you haven't said anything, have you?" She feared Briselle had confided in her sister Georgia or worse, their brothers Westin and Damon.

"I haven't, I swear. They don't know a thing. But sweetie, Marc hasn't changed. In all these years, he's only gotten worse. Him *and* Houston. Don't you think it's time they were cut down?"

"Their time'll come, Bri." Carmen hugged herself to ward off the chill that her other brothers Marcus and Houston always set off. "You're right though. I *have* lived with this *horror* for too long. But that does *not* mean that I'm ready or willing to tell my child whose she is."

"Oh Carmen, you don't even know that for sure-never had the nerve to find out."

"Bri-"

"You have no right to keep it from her now. Belle's a grown woman. She and Isak have been married four years. I'm willing to bet they're thinking of children-"

A Lover's Shame

"Lord Bri, why are you pushing this?!" Carmen swatted the edge of the stainless steel sink with the damp dish cloth she clutched. "Don't you see that it'd destroy her to know?"

"It's destroying you and you *don't* know. What's worse, Carm?"

"What's worse? Worse, is telling the child I treasure that she's here because of that bastard Marcus." Carmen almost choked on the emotion filling her throat. "How do I tell my heart that she's here because my brother raped me?"

Sabella was still smiling. She didn't even realize her lips were tilted upward until she brought her hand to her mouth. The hand lowered eventually, but the rest of her was set rigidly into place. She could feel her eyes stretched wide and growing wider still as the meaning of Carmen's words saturated her brain.

The lowering hand braced against the wall in the corridor outside the kitchen where she'd overheard the conversation between her mother and aunt.

Blindly, she let her hand trail the wall. It guided her as she turned at a snail's pace and headed back the way she came.

SECOND PROLOGUE

What felt like the tip of a boot connected with his side and Marcus Ramsey smothered a groan. *God no more,* he actually prayed. Had he ever called out for help? Most likely not. After all, it was *he* who made others call for help, right? That wasn't true now and would probably never be true again.

Had it been months? Years? He'd lost track of the time. He had lived in hell, a hell he'd often threatened to send others to, but not one he actually believed existed.

It existed. This hell was real and he had been an unwilling guest for what seemed to be; and probably would be, an eternity.

The boot struck his side again and this time Marc's groan would not be silenced. He wondered what new form of torture he'd be subjected to this time? A new form of beating? Another rape? He squeezed his eyes shut. His life passed like a blur in his mind as it often did these days. He cried out apologies, prayers and pleas for forgiveness in the dark cell where they kept him.

He didn't expect forgiveness of course. He had done so much- *too* much- things that would haunt him until his captors decided to be merciful and kill him.

"Up Ramsey!" A male voice ordered.

Seconds later, Marc felt hands beneath his arm pits and he was dragged to his bare feet.

"Stand now or bend later," another man whispered in Marc's ear.

He obeyed as every nerve ending cried out in agony. He struggled, yet managed to remain upright.

"You've got a visitor."

The announcement stirred the first glimpses of hope in Marc's bruised and blood-shot eyes. He knew there was no reason for it, but just the sparse possibility made his heart leap.

A door clanged open and then he blinked twice to assure himself that it was no mirage.

"Carmen?"

Carmen Ramsey's smile was as soft and adoring as a younger sister's should be when she reached out to smooth the back of her hand across her brother's cheek.

Marcus bowed his head and began to cry. "Carm… help me. Help me, please."

"Oh Marc…Honey why should I?" Her tone of voice practically mirrored the sweetness of her smile.

"You- you're my sister." He all but sputtered the words in an effort to speak over the sobs.

Carmen's smile lost none of its graceful allure. The smile remained even as she pulled her hand from her brother's face and returned it in a backhand slap that sent him to his knees.

She stooped close and without a care for the chic eggshell pantsuit she sported. "I'm your sister?" Something cold and amused filled her wide stare as she watched him gasp and cough. "If only that were true Marc…if only you'd allowed me to simply be your sister instead of forcing me to become your lover."

Marcus went deathly still and Carmen's smile took on a grave intensity. Rising in one fluid motion, she turned to the men in the room and nodded.

"Do it," she ordered.

ONE

Near Diamond Peak, Oregon~ 7 years later...

The early morning hour seemed much later as the wicked looking clouds above delivered their rain over Southwest Oregon. Blinding sheets of water darkened the area to an almost pitch black, but that didn't prompt the driver of the heavy duty Dodge Ram to burn its lights. With a stealthy grace, the truck rounded the hauntingly curved private road. The road snaked through the mountain range moving toward the compound that was carved inside and unknown to many.

Chris Orondi rolled his eyes toward the man seated behind the driver's seat. "There he is." He told his partner.

Boyd Eakes nodded. His eyes never left the rear view as the shadow of the hulking truck rounded the bend in the road that dipped several miles below the ground's surface.

"You gonna tell him?" The nervous tinge to Chris's voice was a perfect match to the look in his eyes. He only needed to bite his nails to complete the look of a man scared witless.

"He probably already knows." Boyd's smile was grim as he listened to Chris's shuddery intakes of breath.

Chris wasn't silent for long. "You think he'll blame us?"

Boyd's resulting shrug barely put a wrinkle in the gray ski jacket he wore. "Guess he can do whatever the hell he wants."

"Shit…shit…" Chris rubbed damp hands across the denim covering his thighs. "Well we can't control where she goes, right? I mean…he can't come down on us for that, right? Right?"

Boyd zipped his jacket. "Guess we're about to find out."

Chris pressed back against the cushioned passenger seat and took time to recite a brief prayer. The truck came to a stop next to the Chrysler 300 where Chris and Boyd waited. The driver didn't shut down the engine, but left it purring. The sound did nothing to soothe Boyd's and Chris's nerves. Reluctantly, they left the car.

The rain continued to blow in heavy tufts that had the men raising hands to their faces as though they were working to shield the sun's rays. The tinted driver's side window of the truck eased down as they approached.

Boyd nodded. "Pike."

A Lover's Shame

Chris cleared his throat. "Pike," the cleared throat did nothing to mask the unease in his voice.

Pike Tesano barely shifted his stare toward the men in his employ.

Boyd recognized that it was best to just get to the point. "Thanks for comin' out."

"You called, didn't you?" Despite the wind and rain filling the air with sound, Pike's quiet voice seemed to carry on its own frequency.

"Right, um…" Boyd saw fit to clear *his* throat that time. "She's here."

"How long?"

"Not long." Chris piped up, obviously pleased by that insignificant fact. "We called you the minute we realized where she was headed."

Not impressive, considering their present location was the only sign of *civilization* for miles. The remark even stirred the beginnings of a smirk on Pike's face. Movement from the entrance of the base of the mountain however, stilled him. Without a care for the rain or the men who stood next to the truck, he swung open the door and stepped down.

His eyes; set deep beneath a sleek pair of long dark brows, narrowed towards her as she raced through the rain and into the car waiting a few feet from the entrance. Her car door slammed in tandem with his fist hitting the truck's hood. Her being there angered him almost as much as the fact that she was leaving.

The gesture sent Chris's heavy-set frame in to a shudder. His already shaken nerves were freshly rattled. In spite of Boyd tugging the hem of his all-weather coat to keep him quiet, Chris began to ramble.

"…and we didn't even know she knew the way out here or that she knew her way around in Oregon for Christsakes. She doesn't have any family out here, does she? We know we shoulda called you sooner but; like I said, we didn't even know she-"

Without warning, Pike turned and planted his fist to the center of Chris's considerable gut.

"Quiet." He urged and then turned a hooded stare on Boyd who raised his hands defensively while backing away.

Pike started for the direction of the entrance to the compound.

"Should we keep following her?" Boyd took his courage by the tail and asked.

Pike didn't break stride and Boyd figured it'd be safer (and healthier) to err on the side of caution and maintain the tail.

"Let's get the hell out of here." Boyd nudged Chris; who was leaning against the truck and working to recover from the blow to his abdomen.

The men made quick work of leaving the parking lot.

What the hell was she doing here? Pike asked himself the closer he got to the entrance. God knows he never thought she'd remember the way based on one trip. Then again, she made her living in a profession where attention to the tiniest detail was key and she was tops in her profession.

Despite the wind and rain whipping with frenzy, a scent of her perfume still lingered on the air. The fragrance threatened to send him to his knees and he braced a hand to the granite wall when he neared the dwelling. The weakness lasted but a moment. Rather than focus on how much he missed and wanted his ex wife, he opted to lean on the rage that had ruled him since the day she'd begged him to let her go.

"Dammit Bess! I said no more interruptions!" Brogue Tesano didn't bother to turn when he heard the single booming thud to his office door. He turned in time for his cousin to take his throat into a vice grip and squeeze.

"What was she doing here?" Pike brought his face close to Brogue's, smirking menacingly and squeezing tighter with every word he uttered.

"I…" Brogue couldn't keep his eyes open and knew struggling would only make the man more vicious. "Don't… know…" he managed, curving a hand about his cousin's wrist. "Don't-"

Pike rammed him down on the desk and appeared to be toying with the idea of whether to choke the life from Brogue or to release him. Reluctantly, he chose the latter.

Brogue sputtered, fingers tearing at the neckline of his burgundy crew sweater. He coughed and gasped for breath, yet managed to scramble from the desk before Pike could grab him again.

"Listen to me, man! Listen!" Brogue held his hands outstretched and breathed deep when Pike stopped.

"I didn't know she was comin' out here. I swear it."

Leaning over the desk now littered with pens, maps and papers, Pike set his fists to the surface and kept his head bowed for the longest time.

"Why was she here?" The question sounded harsh and animalistic.

There wasn't much that rattled Brogue Tesano. Seeing his once laid back, good natured and favorite cousin turn into the virtual madman before him, was enough to give him more than a few restless nights.

He cleared his throat. It was only to buy time as he silently debated over how much to share with the man who stood soaking wet in his office. Water dripped from Pike's black ankle-length coat and the shirt and trousers beneath it. His hair hung like shimmering snakes that fell into his lightly bearded and murderously angry face.

Losing his taste for patience, Pike pushed off the desk and made another move for his cousin.

"Alright! Alright!" Brogue shifted to the opposite end of the desk. "She's trying to find her mother."

Pike's hard gaze softened suddenly as if laughter was on the horizon. "And she came to you?" Obvious disbelief filtered the question.

Brogue had to smile as well. "I asked her the same thing," he drew a hand through the lush, honey blonde locks in disarray over his head. "She thinks it might be something shady goin' on and doesn't want her family getting wind of it unless there's something to get riled up about."

Pike scooped wet hair off his forehead and straightened. "What'd you tell her?"

"We didn't spend much time talking about it." Brogue shrugged. "She was in a rush to meet with some folks from her play."

Pike was stroking his whiskered jaw in what appeared to be an absent manner. His eyes however, were sharp as he regarded his cousin. "Who gave the order to kill Yvonne Wilson?"

A Lover's Shame

Brogue stiffened. Direct. That was one aspect of the man's persona that had remained true to form. Pike had always been direct- perhaps why he was so revered on both sides of the family. Direct, honest and with a new found wicked streak the length of the Rio Grande. A combination like that was hard; if not impossible, to outmatch. Of course, Brogue knew his cousin hadn't just plucked the unexpected question out of thin air.

"Uncle Rome," he groaned and massaged the bridge of his nose while referring to Pike's father Roman Tesano. The man had sworn off involvement with the 'dark side' of the family decades ago. His continued knowledge of its inner workings however, was a mystery within a mystery.

"I don't have all night, B." Pike warned, arms now folded over his damp coat.

Brogue decided a *little* directness couldn't hurt. "I was given the order."

"Hmph. So I gather. Who?"

"Pike I can't just-"

"Who?"

"Now wait a minute. This is a messy situation-"

"Just like your face if you don't tell me what I want to know."

Brogue worked his square jaw and debated only a second longer. "You know who she was married to?"

Pike shrugged. "Cufi Muhammad."

"And did you know she was blackmailing certain members of this family?"

Phony shock lent an air of softness to Pike's provocative features. "Blackmail?" He grinned. "Folks in *this* family? You're joking."

Brogue raised his hands to concede to the idiocy of the statement. "She was using those card keys. I'm sure your frat brother Quest Ramsey, if not your father, told you about them?" His blue gaze narrowed, studying Pike's face for confirmation. "Anyway, uncle Vale and my dad were on two of them."

"That's it?" Pike spread his hands. "Uncle Vale's and Uncle Gabe's pictures on those keys are why she was killed?"

"That's right."

"That's stupid. Once the keys were destroyed that would've been that. It'd have been their word against hers. Why kill her?"

Brogue shook his head and looked away then. There wasn't much more he could say without venturing into dangerous and fatal territory. There was only one way to curb the discussion.

"Anyway, you were asking about Belle?" He coolly inquired, witnessing the transformation of his cousin's demeanor. Another thing that had not changed was that the mere mention of Sabella Ramsey's name could shift Pike's focus from the most vital issues.

Brogue pretended not to notice the affect his words had on the man. "She told me her play had some Portland dates. She made a quick trip down here hoping I could… help her." He trailed his finger along the shellacked edge of his desk, before taking a seat on the corner. "She left her card…" he spotted it beneath some papers.

Pike reached over and snatched the card from Brogue's grasp. He left then without as much as a goodbye.

Brogue closed his eyes and bowed his head as a wave of relief claimed him.

***

The pair of headlights in her rearview kept a lengthy yet noticeable distance. The sight of them brought a smile to Belle's face. For the first time in the ten months; since she realized she was being followed, she celebrated the presence of her *shadow*. It took her mind off her mother-or rather, her mother's disappearance. Brogue hadn't been much help, but she hadn't expected him to be.

Her brief smile flashed again and she tightened her grip on the steering wheel while recalling the visit. Shaking her head, she remembered the pitiful explanation he gave for his name showing up on Carmen's phone. He was interested in attaching his name to one of the political events she sponsored throughout the year for a number of senators and congressmen/women in the Pacific North and Southwest.

The humor of the situation faded for Belle then. She'd told him she'd be back but suspected another visit would be a waste of her time. If Brogue Tesano knew anything of her mother's whereabouts, his lips were sealed good and tight. All she could do was continue to wait, worry and wonder. She hadn't seen or heard from her mother since her cousin's wedding three weeks earlier.

The thought of going to her family had occurred to her, but things were just starting to settle down for them. No sense in riling them for no good reason. Her mother could simply be taking a much needed and well-deserved vacation.

Belle leaned her head back against the rest and felt the smile return to her lips. For the first time in so long, the Ramseys were at ease and truly happy. She wanted it to last a little longer, that's all.

The smile wavered and eventually vanished when she thought of her own happiness or the lack thereof.

A Lover's Shame

At any rate, she was at least living her dream costume designing for a hit play. She supposed she was happy enough. But then, did she really deserve to be? After the shameful way she cast aside the best thing in her life, did she really deserve happiness?

Besides, Isak Tesano was the only thing- the only one who had ever made her completely happy and she'd ruined him. She could see it in the brilliant depths of his dark eyes when she told him their marriage was over. She'd killed something inside him.

Her rented black Lexus swerved then and Belle shifted focus back to the rain-slicked road. Dammit! She'd had the man on her mind since her mother mentioned him at Fernando and Contessa's wedding. Then again, he was never very far from her thoughts anyway.

Sabella cast another glance toward the lights in her rearview. For a time, she indulged in the fantasy that he was there…following her in the night on the lonely, twisting road.

***

The cast and crew of the acclaimed hit play *Cab Crew* met for an impromptu celebration at their hotel. Despite outstanding performances to sell out audiences, the group had been working under a storm cloud worrying over how much longer they'd be able to keep the show going on a now fledgling budget.

Having been independently produced, the play hit hard times when the producers' wallets took substantial hits in the financial markets where they made their *real* money. The play's writer and director were sure they'd have to close which meant seeing close to fifty people without jobs.

Then; like the sun bursting through on a rainy day, the play gods intervened. A generous benefactor had come

to their rescue. Following their Oregon dates and a brief
hiatus, *Cab Crew* would hit the road for a new ten month
U.S. tour.

The long, rainy drive had calmed Belle somewhat.
She arrived at the Hotel Surrat envisioning a hot shower
and having a platter of tea and toast sent up to her room. It
took her less than five minutes to discover that the very
appealing plan would have to wait.

"Ms. Ramsey, thank God." The harried looking
front desk clerk typed something into her computer and
then fixed Sabella with a smile. "They've been waiting and
worrying about you for over an hour."

Belle's hands stilled on the belt of her trench coat.
"Waiting? Who?"

"Your colleagues," patience filtered the young
woman's pale blue eyes and she clasped her hands atop the
glossy pine desk. "They're waiting for you at the Inlet Pub,
hotel mezzanine." She pointed upward.

"For what?"

The young woman shrugged, but maintained her
polite demeanor. "Some event- a celebration."

"For what?" Belle tried not to let her frustration
show and brushed fingers across a faint throb near her
temple.

"I only know that they're celebrating- not sure
what." The clerk leaned closer to the desk. "Mr. Prince and
Mr. Victors have been here twice already asking if you'd
checked in."

Frowning then, Belle checked her phone- once
she'd dug it out from her bag. There were over ten
messages from the play's writer Arthur Prince and director
Martin Victors.

A Lover's Shame

Belle muttered an inaudible curse, the full curve of her mouth now twisted into a grim line. She'd kept the phone on vibrate *as usual* and in its *usual* place in the depths of her leather tote. Most of the group had opted to travel together; or as close together as possible, for the Portland dates. Belle had decided to take her trip separately. Thoughts of visiting Brogue first were her top priority.

"Where'd you say this pub is?" Her tone was weary and it took some effort to reciprocate the politeness the clerk had shown.

The woman appeared sympathetic and pointed again. "Just down that hall are the elevators- the M button will take you right there."

"Thank you." Belle hooked the tote strap over her shoulder.

"Oh Ms. Ramsey!" The clerk called when Belle had taken two steps away from the desk. She disappeared for a second or three before returning with what looked like a dark hand towel.

"For your hair," she explained smiling towards the drenched locks plastered to Belle's trench coat.

It was the first time Belle realized she was soaked from the rain. Worry for her mother and thoughts over what her ex-husband's cousin *wouldn't* tell her, had consumed the better part of her common sense. At least she'd thought enough to cover up she grimaced and tightened the belt on the black ankle-length trench.

"Thank you." Belle shook the towel and managed a faint smile. She was about to set off again when she recalled her bag on the front desk. "Is there anything to sign before checking in?" She asked, realizing that piece of business had slipped her mind as well.

AlTonya Washington

The clerk was already waving her hand. "We'll take care of it Ms. Ramsey. Just go have fun with your friends and get warmed up."

Sabella figured warming up would at least be do-able. Having fun with her friends… only if she could shut down her brain's *worry* mode.

She walked into the Inlet Pub drying her hair. The chestnut brown waves rippled down her back in a glossy tumble each time she drew the thick towel through them. Her movements were as absent as the look in her gaze which narrowed when she heard her name cutting through the mellow music coloring the establishment.

Absent-minded or not, Belle couldn't help but smile at the sight of Martin Victors rushing towards her. Short and stout, the man had more confidence and charisma than men twice his height and half his size.

Martin was also a chauvinist and proud of it. When he hired Belle, he as much as told her that he was giving her the job as his new costume designer because she was 'damned good to look at' first and because her work was exquisite second.

That was almost four years ago and they'd been great friends ever since. *Cab Crew* was the latest in a long line of plays they had collaborated on. Martin's boisterous and protective persona reminded Belle so much of her rowdy male cousins. She'd felt at home from her first day of rehearsals on their earlier plays.

Unfortunately, Martin Victors wasn't full of his usual smiles and cheer that evening.

"Just where've you been?" He scolded, the elaborately tied scarf bumped against his stomach as he bolted over. "Do you know how worried we were?" He stood before her, tapping a designer loafer shod foot as he fumed.

Sabella leaned down to kiss the man's balding head. "Have you forgotten I grew up in Seattle? It's not my first time visiting Oregon. I know my way around well enough."

Martin dismissed the explanation with a wave and roll of his eyes. "You're too gorgeous to be out and about alone on a rainy night. Besides, you have a group of people here and ready to get on with the celebrating."

Belle pulled the towel through her hair again. "Exactly what are we celebrating?"

"Salvation!"

She felt herself being tugged back against the owner of the jovial voice. Arthur Prince planted a loud kiss to her cheek.

"We're on the road for another ten months."

"Was there some reason that we wouldn't be?" Belle cast a sideways glance toward Arthur. The *look* passing between the writer and director did not go unnoticed.

Arthur's thin frame stiffened in response to the knowing look on her face. His fair features were equally stiff when he glared at Martin. "Would you please tell her already?"

Martin bristled before conceding. "Sorry Hon."

"An apology?" Belle pushed a hand into her coat pocket. "This must be *really* bad."

"There was no need for you to know about our money woes." Martin tugged the hem of his tailored suit coat.

Sabella stood silently waiting for the full explanation which Martin shared after another moment of bristling.

"I can't believe you'd keep quiet about this- not only from me but from everyone else. We have a right to know if we're about to lose our paychecks Martin."

"You're the only one we didn't tell, love." Arthur cleared his throat and went to stand behind Martin when Belle turned on him.

"Why didn't you come to *me* for the money?" She hung her head the minute the words left her mouth. Martin's offense to the question was quite obvious.

"You work for us Ms. *Ramsey. We* pay *you*. Not the other way around."

"Oh…" Arthur patted the top of Martin's shiny head and then moved to give Belle another squeeze. "Let's not get our feathers ruffled over money. It's tacky." He gave an indignant tug to the flowing cuffs of the flamboyant linen shirt he sported. "We weren't completely on the skids, beautiful. We were saved before things got really dismal." He winked slyly.

"Well…" Belle's mood wasn't completely eased, but she was happy things had worked out. She fixed Martin with a challenging stare and slapped both hands to her sides. "Are you allowed to tell me how you turned things around?"

Martin's demeanor transformed and he beamed under his heavy tan. "We'll do better than *tell* you, we'll *show* you."

Each man offered an arm and escorted Belle through a maze of candlelit tables. When they stopped near one, Belle was ever thankful for the support of her escorts.

Arthur waved a hand toward the man who stood. "Sabella Ramsey, meet our generous benefactor, Mr. Isak Tesano."

TWO

Pike watched his ex-wife bask in the fair amount of shock that he knew was claiming her then. It had virtually consumed him when she walked into the pub during his conversation with *Cab Crew*'s writer and director. He'd never been able to focus on much when she was in his sight anyway. Her presence- hell, the simple mention of her name was enough to re-task his brain onto one topic: her.

He nodded towards one of the chairs at the table. "Have a seat…Ms. Ramsey." Were his first words to her in over seven years.

As though she were hypnotized, Belle followed his instructions. Blinking madly, she looked everywhere except his striking face.

Pike watched her wringing the towel she'd been using to dry her hair. He indulged in a second to enjoy the sight of the damp wavy mass framing her very lovely pecan brown face. He then looked to Martin Victors in a silent message for him to begin.

Martin and Arthur found nothing strange in Isak Tesano's *observance* of their colleague. They themselves had often been struck speechless by their enchanting designer.

"Mr. Tesano's foundation reached out with an offer."

"A very generous offer," Arthur chimed in, straightening proudly in his seat.

Martin nodded. "We'd have been fools not to accept it."

Belle risked a glance in Pike's direction then. She blinked away quickly when she found his dark bottomless gaze set on her. She prayed for something to say before Martin or Arthur grew concerned by her behavior. No one on the play knew she'd been married once. She'd been very blessed in being able to keep her private life- private.

"Do you dance, Ms. Ramsey?"

When Belle looked at him that time her breath caught and held. She couldn't ignore what dwelled in his voice and eyes. She'd never seen it before. It had never been there before. It was predatory. It was lethal and it was wounded. Yes- she recalled her thoughts from earlier that evening- she had ruined him.

"Well of course she dances!" Martin burst in with contagious laughter filling his voice.

Pike stood and began to make his way round the table.

Belle looked quickly toward Martin and Arthur. Somehow she managed a brief smile for them before she stood. She reached out to take the hand Pike offered but he withdrew it and gave another slow nod instead.

"I think your coat'll be fine here at the table," he said.

Martin and Arthur laughed. Arthur stood to assist. Belle missed the disapproval flash in Pike's gaze when she eased out of the trench. The dress she wore beneath it was a casual yet chic cobalt blue number that accentuated her thick, curvaceous 5"11 frame.

Pike had masked his displeasure (somewhat) by the time he offered his hand again. Sabella pressed her lips together when her fingers touched his palm. She could have swooned and cried in the same moment over the memories evoked by that single, simple touch.

God, please don't let me fall flat on my face, she prayed.

Falling on her face would have been easy to do when he pulled her snug against him on the dance floor. The music had changed from its *up*beat to something more sensual. Belle wondered whether the quartet had instinctively known what Pike wanted.

Still, she wasn't sure whether his arms about her were a blessing or a curse. Sure, the embrace kept her on her feet, but it wreaked unimaginable havoc on her hormones. Thoroughly unnerved, she rested her hands on his upper arms beneath the gray shirt open at the collar and hanging outside his dark trousers. Helpless to resist, she closed her eyes and inhaled the appealing scent of his cologne.

"What have you done to yourself?"

The abrupt question jerked Belle from her daze. She forced herself to look up at him then.

"What?" She didn't begrudge the tiny sound of her voice knowing she could produce nothing stronger.

Pike offered no verbal response. Instead, he merely supplied a proprietary pat to the very full curve of her bottom filling out the dress.

Then, she could easily read the look in his radiant midnight stare and knew exactly what he was questioning.

"I um…I lost a little weight."

"What the hell for?" He growled without a second's hesitation.

Belle looked away to shield the smile that fought to appear on her mouth. That part of him hadn't changed. He'd once told her that not only did he want to *see* what he touched but he wanted to *feel* it too. She could remember asking if he'd be happy if she were a thousand pounds. He never gave her an answer, he only smiled.

"Well?"

"I um," she shook her head searching for a reply. "I've only gone down one dress size."

The answer didn't please him. "You're lying." His arms flexed about her waist.

"Isak…" she sighed, missing the way he was affected by it. "It was two sizes and you can't really tell."

"*I* can tell."

"What are you doing here?" The banter between them had loosened her tongue enough to ask.

"I talked to Martin about meeting up here when the crew arrived for the Portland shows." He glided both hands over her hips, smirking when he noticed her swallow with effort. "We were waiting for you to get here. Took you long enough."

"I…"

"Yes…?"

"I had a stop to make."

Of course Pike knew all too well about her *stop*. He'd been on his way down to meet with Martin and Arthur when he'd gotten the call that she was on her way to see his cousin.

"How'd you know about the play? That it was in trouble?" She kept her eyes focused on where his light beard covered the dent in his chin. At that point, she could've cared less about his response. She was more interested in taking in the rich bronze of his complexion now further shadowed by the whiskers covering the lower half of his face.

The beard added something dangerous but just as beautiful to his features. The mane of glossy blue-black he'd once worn clipped short was now longer, more lush and practically brushed his very broad shoulders.

God, please don't let me fall flat on my face, she meditated on the prayer again.

As though he'd heard the silent plea, he tugged her closer and she could feel the strong beat of his heart against her breast. The pumps matching her dress, added several inches to her already stunning height. The heels helped bring her just shy of his eye level.

"The foundation's always looking to donate money to the arts," he was saying though it was clear that his mind wasn't totally focused on the explanation. "When my people came across the play and your connection to it- naturally they came to me."

Belle only nodded.

"Your connection to me is obviously something *your* colleagues aren't aware of." He smoothly noted, brows rising when her nodding ceased and her eyes flew to his face.

"Hmm?" He prompted, hoping like hell he was maintaining the cold mask that; up until he'd seen her, had been easy to keep in place.

Pike had always believed such flowery phrases as *heartache* and *weak in the knees* to be amusing and fictitious. No one could possibly feel that way.

She stood there looking up at him. Her full, kissable mouth was parted as she worked up an explanation. Her wide incredible eyes were fringed with the long lashes that framed them. His heart quite literally…ached.

"It just never came up." Her voice; softer than usual, delivered the first thought that sprang to mind.

"Never came up?"

His voice harbored a fierceness that chilled her. He looked away then and Belle watched him grind down on the muscle along his jaw.

"Let's go." He stopped their minute sway to the slow beat of the music.

"Where?" Her fingers curved into the open collar of his shirt as she braced against him.

He cupped her chin. "Anywhere I damn well like."

Sabella swallowed but refused to budge.

Smiling a smile that had nothing to do with humor, Pike kept his hold on her chin and brought his mouth close to her ear. "How about this, let's go or watch me tell your friends the deal's off."

She pulled back as far as he'd let her. "You couldn't do that."

The humorless smile remained. "I could and in a fuckin' heartbeat." He promised.

***

"So what do I tell her?"

"Anything but where I am."

"Hmph and lucky for me that's the only thing she wants to know."

There was brief silence followed then by soft laughter from the woman on the other end of Brogue's phone line.

"Sweetie…now *you* of all people should have plenty of…reasons at your disposal to use to explain a person's sudden disappearance, hmm?"

Grimacing, Brogue let the barb dig deep. "I understand." Sighing, he swiveled his chair towards the expanse of black beyond his window. "So how long are we supposed to let this bastard linger? He's begging for death every second."

Carmen Ramsey's laughter came through the line loud and robust that time. "Perfect! Lord… who would've thought it? Let's put a recorder down there, alright? I'd like to hear the devil screaming out for some mercy."

It was Brogue's gasp coming over the phone line then. And people accused *him* of being sadistic! Jesus what had happened between these people? He wondered.

"What do I say if I give her my best excuse and she still doesn't buy it?"

Brogue's question was enough to stifle Carmen's amusement.

"You just keep my dear brother alive. Alive and suffering with more still to come when I get back there. And you keep my baby girl away from him- you don't let him near her. You don't want to be on the wrong side of me Brogue."

Brogue massaged the muscles clenched at the nape of his neck. He thought of the man chained in the bowels of his compound several miles below where he sat talking with the woman who wanted him there. No, being on the 'wrong side' of Carmen Ramsey was a place even he didn't want to be.

***

Shallow relief nudged a sigh past Belle's lips when she realized they were heading deeper into the hotel instead of outside it. Her relief was short lived once they were inside the elevator. She and Pike were its only two occupants and she was grateful for the wall railing to lean on. His cologne filled the small confines of the car. It was a different one from when they were married… Still, it called to her as seductively as if he'd spoken to her.

"Can't you look at me, Bella?"

Her hands tightened on the rail when the deep quiet of his voice touched her ears. She kept her eyes on the floor.

To force a reaction, Pike closed the distance between them and crowded her into one corner of the cherry paneled car.

"Can't you?" He probed, tilting his head to watch her face.

The seconds that passed felt more like hours, but she finally managed to look up at him. She leaned deeper into the rail when she saw what was there. Gone, was the coldness in his eyes that she'd witnessed at the table.

Sadly, the encounter was brief. Pike hadn't bothered to push for a floor when they'd entered the car. The doors re-opened in the lobby to admit three more passengers.

"Where to?" He inquired and dutifully hit the buttons to the requested floors.

Sabella watched him also hit the button for the floor to her suite. Again, that brief flutter of relief made its presence known. He was taking her to *her* room, not his. The relief fled more quickly when another possibility intruded. Perhaps, he had a mind to stay the night.

They were alone again when the car hit her floor. The doors opened and; with hands settled in the deep pockets of his trousers, Pike simply leaned against one side of the opened doors and waited for her to exit.

Key in hand, Belle relied on the foolish hope that he'd leave her with a goodnight. Hmph. Foolish indeed.

He stood several inches behind her and patiently waited. His presence was like the sun- not close enough to touch but impossible to ignore.

Sabella didn't turn when the door opened. She walked on into the suite, tossed her things to a chair and waited for him to follow.

"What were you doing out at Brogue's?" He slammed the door shut behind him.

Belle whirled around to face him. She was about to ask how he knew, but stifled the question. Instead, she put a knowing smile in place. "Right... I guess I underestimated how good the men you have following me are."

Pike smiled then too yet fought the urge to laugh over her mistaken summation. "They have their moments. How long have you known?"

Belle took a moment to think it over. Absently, she ran her hands across her hips and missed his pitch stare helplessly following the movement.

"I spotted them at the opening performance for the new season almost ten months ago. Center section. Row H."

Attention to detail indeed. Pike silently admired how sharp she still was. He wouldn't let the softness linger though. "You were saying about Brogue?"

Belle shrugged, figuring it made no sense to hide it. "I haven't seen or heard from my mother since Fernando's wedding three weeks ago. I saw Brogue's name on Mama's phone when she left it behind at the hotel we shared during the wedding. I went to ask Brogue about it."

"What'd he say?" Pike sat on the back of the sofa and folded his arms across his chest.

Belle shook her head. "Not much. Something about wanting to donate money for a benefit Mama might host next year."

"I'm guessing you didn't believe him." He had to smile at her expression. "I don't blame you. The fool lies as easily as he breathes. Will you let him off the hook about it?"

"I don't see why I shouldn't." She fingered a lock of her hair. "There may be nothing to it. I've been calling her three times a week for the last three weeks. She could just be taking a vacation. Lord knows she could use one."

Eyes narrowing, Pike tilted back his head. "Is she alright?"

"I guess…" Belle paced the area near the room's floor to ceiling windows. "She's been distant though- not in a bad way but like… she's got a secret she's dying to tell but it's more fun to hide it." She shook her head as though the explanation made no sense. She focused her attention beyond the rain-sprinkled windows.

Pike focused on his hands clenching and unclenching into fists. "Why didn't you go to the guys?"

Mention of her cousins brought a smile to Belle's pecan brown face. "They're all so happy- been through so much with everything that's come out." She traced an invisible pattern onto the window. "I didn't want to bother them about something that could be nothing."

For a time, the only sound in the room was the rain hitting the windows. As Sabella stood there focused on the night, Pike dropped his guard. He did away with the cold mask and absorbed the sight of her. He dwelled on how much he missed her. How much he wanted her back in every way. When she glanced across her shoulder at him, he easily set the chill back into place.

"Why didn't you come to me?"

"Why?"

The 'chill' went to downright frigid. Sabella took an unconscious step backward at the sight of his glare.

"It'd be in your best interest to be where I can find you." He'd moved from the sofa and towards her. "Don't get any ideas of heading back to Vancouver anytime soon."

The almond brown pools of her eyes widened at his mention of the place she now called home. Sabella noticed his barely there smile and narrowed gaze that dared her to question him. Whatever urge she had to do so was quickly tamped down.

Pike watched, awed by the manner in which she controlled herself. "I suggest you not call my bluff on this," he said deciding to test the depths of her self control. "Otherwise your friends'll damn well find themselves looking for a new benefactor."

The threat *did* create a tiny fissure in the controlled wall about her emotions. She moved closer with challenge sparkling in her stare. "I could keep that play afloat easy."

"Right. Martin would sooner take money from the devil."

As Belle studied her ex's sinfully seductive features, she wondered if Martin hadn't done exactly that.

A Lover's Shame

Pike bowed his head while closing the last few steps that separated them. His cologne teased her nose again. He'd moved so close, she thought *hoped* he'd intended to kiss her.

His intentions weren't so sweet.

"Is that the way you treat folks you...care about? Do you intend to shame Martin and Arthur into having to accept a handout from their wealthy employee?"

Shame. Belle turned away the second she heard the word.

Pike didn't argue her reaction. Her back toward him gave him another chance to drop his hard, guarded expression. God, he'd prayed the night would have gone much more differently than it had.

Like an idiot, he'd hoped buying into her play would forge a bond that would...what? Get them back together? *Stupid!* His features tightened again.

He hadn't counted on Carmen Ramsey going missing and even less on Belle going to Brogue for answers. Even more suspicious was the fact that Brogue hadn't mentioned those calls to his ex-mother-in-law. Pike studied Belle for another few moments then; without another word, he left and let the door slam behind him.

THREE

Sabella woke the next morning hoping the previous
evening had been part of some weird dream. The sun was
fighting to get past the eggshell drapes in the bedroom of
her suite. She scrambled from the bed and sprinted over to
pull them from in front of the windows. Puddles of water
from the storm rested along the window sill and platforms.

She knew she'd been lying to herself. She *hadn't*
hoped it was all part of some dream. She'd wanted it to be
real. Dreams had nothing on reality.

A Lover's Shame

    The way his arms felt around her, the way he felt beneath her fingertips as they danced, the sound of his soft, deep voice. If ever she'd wondered whether time had diminished her love for him, she'd gotten her answer last night.

    She'd never stopped loving him- never would. But he didn't need what she could possibly bring to the table. He was too good to settle for that. Or, at least he *had* been too good before her shame had ruined him.

    She smirked, staring without really seeing the view of downtown Portland beyond the tall windows. Such irony... she left so her shame wouldn't touch him and she wound up damaging him anyway.

    The grinding sound of the cell phone broke into Belle's thoughts. She celebrated the vibrating interruption and moved quickly to grab it from the night table. Sudden laughter filled the room when she saw Sabra's name.

    "Good morning." Belle greeted her cousin.

    There was brief hesitation over the line. "Yes, it is. *Morning*, that is. I'd say it's way better than... *good* for you." Sabra's husky tone held a curious undercurrent.

    "What?" Belle laughed.

    "Things must be going good with the play. You sound like you're on cloud nine."

    Belle tapped her fingers to her mouth and considered the observation. "Well..." she blinked, unable to focus on the words she needed. "I...."

    "Yes...?"

"Well, I don't think I sound any more or less *happy* than usual."

"If you say so. Anyway, I'm only calling because I didn't hear from you last night and you promised to call when your plane landed."

"Oh Sabi…" Belle flopped back on the bed and rested the back of her hand to her forehead. "I'm sorry. Last night was just so strange."

"Strange? Something with the flight?"

"No um," Belle worried the pearly buttons on her sleep shirt.

"Listen, you're gonna have to give over some clarification- talkin' about *strange things* in Portland of all places."

Belle rolled her eyes. "Vegas isn't the only exciting place in the world."

"So *you* say." Sabra countered and then sighed dramatically. "So I've got a free morning and ready to chat about your *strange* night. What'sup?"

"I…went to see Brogue."

Silence filled the line again, but Sabella knew it was more than a brief hesitation on her cousin's part.

"This is why I didn't want to talk about it." She said.

"Well um," Sabra's sigh that time was a bit less airy. "What'd you go see him for?"

"I saw his name on Mama's phone when we were out for Fernando's wedding."

"Brogue's calling Aunt Carmen?"

"Yeah," Belle braced up on an elbow. "He said he just wanted to talk to her about linking his name to one of her charity events."

"Brogue's interested in charity?"

"You don't believe him?"

"I didn't say that."

"Then-"

"Just don't be so quick to think his reasons are... bad."

"And what could possibly make me think that?" Belle pushed up to sit in the middle of the tangled bed. "Sabi are you forgetting all we know about him? He's not the same guy you knew in college."

"Right," Sabra didn't blow up over her cousin's mention of her ancient *acquaintance* with Brogue Tesano.

Belle closed her eyes and knocked a fist to her head. "Honey…"

"It's okay Belle, it's okay- I'm good."

"I'm sorry anyway. I wasn't trying to take you back there."

"I know but… it's just he wasn't always like that. He was thrown into a lot of nasty shit that he never saw comin'."

"Hmph," Belle lay back against the pillows lining the headboard. "Haven't we all been?" She groaned.

"Sorry girl," Sabra chuckled after a moment. "We're just screwin' up each other's mornings all over the place, aren't we? Anyway… you really did sound happy when you answered the phone."

"Well you said it yourself- the play's doing well."

"Oh… right…"

Belle frowned, dreading the woman's passive yet probing tone. "What?" She grimaced over her inability to resist questioning it.

"Guess I just thought it might have somethin' to do with Pike."

"Why would you think that?" Belle scrambled off the bed for a second time that morning.

Sabra gave into an unexpected giggle. "Damn… am I still the only one who can make you lose it like that? Or was it my mention of your sexy ex?"

"Cut the shit Sabra. How do you know I've seen him?"

"Ooooh!" Sabra's drawl could rival that of the smallest child's. "I swear I didn't know. So *that's* why you sound so giddy." She giggled wickedly. "To hell with cloud nine. Cloud *ninety-nine* is where you reside when Mr. Isak Tesano's in your world."

"Sabra…" Belle massaged the bridge of her nose.

"Honey I'm sorry. I meant it when I said I didn't know and I'm sorry for teasing. Smoak booked the top floor of my first tower."

"Oh…"

"Yeah…"

Belle sat on the cushioned window seat. "Is he there?"

"No, he's just got the floor *on hold.*"

A Lover's Shame

"Hmph. I'm impressed that you're not jumpin' off the deep end over that one."

"Please don't put the halo over my head yet. I've gone off plenty. Just ask Quay and Ty," Sabra admitted, referring to their cousin and his wife. "Anyway…that's why I asked about Pike."

"So what are you thinking?" Belle asked while holding her thumbnail between her teeth.

"Girl, you don't want to know. I've got a mind for business but I lack the appropriate psychiatric credentials to go probin' around inside a man's head. Hell, it gives me the shivers to even think about what mess could be brewing up in there."

Belle's laughter filled the room again. "Are we speaking of Smoak Tesano's brain exclusively?"

Sabra sucked her teeth. "Sadly no. I think they're all a bunch of idiots. Our loving cousins included."

"So *do* you think something's up? Seriously Sabra?'

"I got a weird vibe from Ty when they came out for the parties. Maybe Quay said something- I don't know… Only time will tell. Personally, I hope I'm wrong. I can only speak for myself in sayin' that I've had enough with nasty shit being thrown my way and never see it comin'."

Closing her eyes, Belle raked a hand through her hair and groaned. "Haven't we all?"

***

Pike sat outside the barely noticeable entry way to the offices that served to conceal the way into the depths of Brogue's compound. He'd tried to calm himself having had enough of the rage that sent him into fits over the smallest things.

Propping an elbow to the driver's side window he tapped his fingers against the leather braiding around the steering wheel and thought of Belle. The rage had abated as if she'd held out some wand and ordered it back.

Now; two days later, it was back and in full force. Brogue was once again in the cross hairs of his anger. It had taken that long to process everything that had happened- *was* happening and how it all played into what he'd already suspected and recently been made aware of.

Pike closed his eyes and let his head fall back on the rest. Images of Sabella in his mind jousted with the anger trying to maintain dominance. He'd been fighting a losing battle against it over the last seven years. One day, out of the clear blue, the woman he loved more than his life told him they were done. Just like that and he'd actually let her go.

His jaw clenched on the memory which should have been enough to allow the anger to set firmly in place. But now… now he had all these images- *new* images of her in his head. They were powerful and God were they beautiful.

His fingers flexed about the steering when he recalled the way she felt in his hands. He'd spent much of the last two days calling himself a fool for not taking what he craved from her that night.

Soon, he promised himself and looked toward the rock encrusted entrance to Brogue's chamber of horrors. *Soon,* he repeated before leaving the truck.

A Lover's Shame

***

A thick skin was needed if one had plans to work for Brogue Tesano. Bess Frankfurt was the complete opposite of tough and her skin had been anything but thick-more like baby soft. That all changed within a few months of working for her fierce yet 'fair' boss. She'd seen things that should have turned her red hair white.

Instead of running quick, fast and in a hurry, Bess came to embrace the disturbing things she'd seen and facilitated for her boss. And yet…in spite of the 'bad ass' she'd become; listening to the tortured cries of the only *guest* currently accommodated in the depths of the building, she was chilled and nervous as hell.

The man should've been dead by now. He'd been through more than anyone they'd ever kept there. But they wouldn't kill him. Someone wanted this man to suffer a bit longer before he went on to his reward.

Bess wasn't sure if she had the *thick skin* required to witness how they'd choose to send him into the waiting arms of death. She was gulping down her second cup of black coffee when her ears caught the grinding sound of the pulleys on the sliding granite doors. Someone was waiting in their cheery outer office.

Bess wasn't in the mood to greet anyone. However, as it was mid-morning it was probably not actual business but someone who had lost their way.

No, not a wayward visitor Bess realized when she stepped out into the cozy office. This was a deliberate visitor. Better than that, he was a gorgeous one.

"Pike…" She almost purred the man's name when she found him shrugging out of his coat as he crossed the room.

With his considerable charm in place, Pike greeted Brogue's assistant of the last eleven years. "How is it that you always keep yourself looking good enough to eat?" He brushed his mouth across the curve of her jaw.

The smooth flattery worked as intended and Bess blushed the color of her hair. "This is a surprise and a very nice one," she pressed a hand to Pike's chest and scanned his face with pure adoration and sexual heat filling her sea blue gaze. "We rarely get visits from the *other* side of the family and never the *sexy* other side."

Pike's grin came easily. "Don't you find my uncles sexy?"

"Definitely," She gave a tug to the open collar of his shirt. "But *you* get first dibs."

"You do know how to make a man feel good Bess."

Bess kept her grip on his shirt and moved in closer. "You ain't seen nothin' yet."

"I'm tempted," Pike tilted his head and made a pretense of appraising Bess' rail thin frame that somehow managed to fill out the gray satin dress she wore. "I don't think my cousin would approve though and in his place of business."

"*Business?*" Bess rolled her eyes. "The only *business* we have is dealing with that terrible man and his maddening screaming. I'm no fan of Marcus Ramsey's but even *I'm* starting to feel sorry for him." She cast an irritable glance across her shoulder. "I just wish they'd put him out of his misery."

"Well I don't have an appointment with my cousin," Pike remained cool but was more alert then in the wake of Bess's slip. "I really do need to speak with him about Marcus though," he offered an arm, "Care to escort me?"

Bess didn't think of refusing or questioning the delicious Tesano she would have given anything to take to bed- just once. Accepting what she was being offered, she took Pike's arm and led the way.

"Looks like he's comin' around boss. You want us to start in again?"

Brogue cupped one hand beneath his arm pit while the other stroked his jaw. He regarded Otto Fusilli's question with mixed emotion. He'd be the first to argue the payoffs of torture, but what was the benefit here? It wasn't as if they were trying to pull information from the son of a bitch, he thought.

"Fuck it," he said and shrugged off Otto's question. "Our only orders right now are to keep the bastard alive. Besides," his eyes narrowed with devilish intent. "There's gotta be some kind of torture sittin' in your own shit, right?"

The men were still laughing when Bess brought Pike down. Brogue nodded, sending Otto on his way and then he bolted over to his cousin and secretary.

"Thanks love," Pike was saying to Bess leaving her with a tender fist-bump to her chin and a kiss to the temple that she was sure to treasure. He waited until she'd practically floated back into the elevator before turning to Brogue.

"Don't hold her responsible." Pike nodded past his cousin's shoulder. "She thought I knew about what you have goin' on down here."

"You don't need to be here Pike."

"What the hell are *you* doin' with Marc Ramsey when half the world thinks he's dead?"

Brogue focused on rubbing his hands together and sighed. "Half the world thinks he's dead, the other half couldn't give a shit."

"Someone gives a shit." Pike's black stare sharpened with a murderous determination and a fair amount of suspicion. "Whose got you doin' their bidding this time? Uncle Gabe?"

The sound of his father's name roused a muffled oath below Brogue's breath. "Pop doesn't know a thing unless somebody else told him."

Pike bowed his head, directing his voice toward the floor. "Either cease the vague bullshit or let your men watch you get your ass beat." He proposed, fixing his cousin with a look that confirmed his preference to Brogue selecting the latter offer.

Again, Brogue muffled a curse and then waved a hand toward the corridor. "After you," He said.

FOUR

"Carmen Ramsey?" Pike said for the third time since his cousin began the story.

"As in your ex-mother-in-law? Yes." Brogue confirmed for the third time as well.

"And you've had him here all this time because of her?"

"Since Houston Ramsey's trial- the first day of it, that is. Didn't go beyond that, you recall?" Brogue raised a brow.

Leaning forward in his chair, Pike rested elbows to knees and stroked his beard absently. "Perfect timing with all the commotion that day. It's when Houston's wife killed him, right?"

"It's when they *say* his wife killed him."

Pike's eyes shifted to meet Brogue's. "What did you do?"

"What I was told to do."

"Why?" Pike spread his hands and rested back in the chair. "It makes no sense. You're *sure* that it was *Carmen* Ramsey who… *arranged* for her brother and sister-in-law to be killed *and* to have her other brother brought here to your fun house?"

Brogue moved to and fro in the swivel chair he occupied. "Now you're thoroughly informed P. Happy?"

"You still haven't told me *why*? Why'd she do it? Hell, everybody knows Marcus is dirt but what would push his little sister to do this? And turn him over to the Tesano's top death dealer, besides?" Pike didn't notice the tightening of Brogue's features then. "What happened between them?" He asked.

Brogue pulled a hand through his hair and smiled sadly. "I'm willin' to sit here and spout all sorts of theories, cuz. But what I've just told you is all I've got. My employer didn't see fit to clue me in to *all* the details. Now I hope you believe me since I'm not in the mood to have my ass beat just now."

Pike was pacing the dismal, bare surroundings of the small concrete room Brogue had selected for them to

A Lover's Shame

talk. His thoughts churned as he worked to come up with some explanations. He frequently pulled his hands from his pockets and stroked his jaw momentarily before shoving them back inside his jeans.

"The day they died, Houston and Daphne, was it an accident? Did something go wrong? Marc was brought here, why weren't they?" He practically fired the questions at his cousin.

Brogue's sad smile mingled with sympathy. "Sorry man, story won't change no matter how many ways you turn it. Carmen's instructions were to the letter- make her brother and sister-in-law's deaths look like a murder suicide and not a hair on Marc's head was to be touched."

"Hmph," Pike leaned against the wall, "Until he got here, right?"

Brogue mimicked the grin Pike flashed. "I swear we haven't touched one hair on his sweet head. The rest of him however…" Brogue shook his head after a long moment. "I've been tryin' to make sense of her motives and I keep comin' back to one thing- Belle."

Pike moved from the wall. His expression urged his cousin to continue and to be quick about it.

Brogue didn't expect anything less. Besides, he wasn't altogether opposed to having someone to bounce his *theories* off on. He pulled a decanter and two glasses from the last drawer of a beaten metal filing cabinet in the room.

Pike waved, refusing the drink when Brogue clinked the glasses.

"She comes in to…watch the *things* we do to him. Some of the things she's asked us to do…" Brogue shook his head while pouring a generous amount of whiskey into a glass. "We've had to bring in outside *help*. I've seen her come up with ways to torture him on a whim- like it just came to her and she was pickin' it off a shelf. Can you believe that shit?" He downed the whiskey in one swallow.

"And she never told you why?"

"Hmph," Brogue shook his head again. "She says things to him when he's crying out for it to stop." He sloshed more drink into the glass and then set the decanter on top of the file cabinet. "It's fucked up to see a woman that awesome-looking with all that- that hate no…that's not right…*venom* in her expression.

"One of my guys was heading out one day after they were done with him. She was there whispering to him. He must've said something that made her mad because she raised her voice a little. My guy heard her tell him he'd never see *her*, never know what a beauty *she* was. She told him he'd never touch her Belle."

Pike reclaimed his seat on the folding chair nearest the door. After what seemed close to ten minutes, he looked over at his cousin. "It's revenge."

"But what for?" Brogue asked, his glass paused midway to his mouth.

Pike only bowed his head and offered no reply. He hadn't noticed his hands were clenched into fists until a blur of red flashed beneath his line of sight.

A Lover's Shame

"Where is he?" Pike's voice then was a growl tempered by an eerie whisper.

"Here."

"Where, here?"

Brogue's vivid blues narrowed as he realized his error in speaking so casually. "Pike-"

Whatever warning Brogue may've uttered was cut when Pike left the chair like a flash of light. Without conscience or hesitation, he slammed Brogue down to the dented desk which matched the filing cabinet.

"Where?" Pike gripped the man's throat with deadly intentions. He smiled when Brogue sputtered on the breath that was slowly shutting off.

"Hall…" he managed.

Pike eased his grip. Some.

"End of the hall- double doors…"

Pike turned and headed from the cramped room.

"You don't want in on this Pike!" Brogue winced, rubbing his throat as the words scraped it like sandpaper.

It would be useless and very possibly hazardous to his health to try stopping the man. Still, Brogue followed Pike who was running at full tilt down the corridor towards the chrome doors where he kept his lone guest.

Seconds after Pike disappeared past the doors, Brogue watched as two of his men were unceremoniously shoved out.

"You want us to get him outta there, boss?" Otto was breathless and stumbled a tad.

Brogue grimaced. "He'll kill you." He reached for his cell. "I've got a better idea."

Sabella was glad all the costumes and fittings were over and done with. The rate she was going all she would've managed to accomplish was massacring the creations and leaving the cast to deliver their lines in rags.

The day was a sunny one, but there was a definite chill in the air. She'd taken up residence at a rear table in one of the hotel restaurants. She wasn't interested in having breakfast. Instead, she made do for two hours with her sketch pads and a pot of tea from the restaurant kitchen.

At least the tea had been consumed. She'd gotten little use from the sketch pads and pencils since she'd claimed the table and attempted to work. It seemed her interest was more focused on the view past the windows but her thoughts were on Isak. Of course they were on Isak.

Sabella rolled her eyes as her heart did its familiar bump- a given whenever his name was mentioned. She went back to that day- the day everything changed. The day she found out she was the product of a rape. Worse still, she was the product of a rape committed by her uncle on his sister- her mother.

Belle swallowed on the bitter taste at the back of her throat- usual reaction whenever the thought struck her. She'd thought of it more and more since Isak's… reappearance.

That day…it was still so clear in her head. Especially Isak- he was so happy and in love with her and she with him. Now…he was so changed, so angry. The rage rolled off him like sweat and that was all her doing.

The shame she felt over her conception was nothing compared to the shame she felt over what she'd done to him. She could live with that, though. As sorry as she was for ruining the goodness in him, she had to find some way to survive. That was only possible if he didn't know. She wouldn't survive him knowing the violent truth of her. How could he see her as anything but something tainted and ugly then?

Her breath expelled in a single shuddery stream of air. She knew tears were only moments away from showing themselves.

Thankfully, a call was coming through from a private number. She grabbed the phone and answered the call as if the person on the other end were her lifeline. When she heard Brogue's voice, she wondered whether anyone would ever put his name in the same sentence with the word 'lifeline'. She wouldn't have time to debate it for long.

"I need you back out here Belle. ASAP." Brogue didn't waste time with small talk.

"Is it my mother?"

Brief hesitation. "In a manner of speaking," He said.

Belle shut down the phone and left the table seconds later.

***

Seattle, Washington~

Quest Ramsey and Taurus Ramsey were leaning on opposite ends of a pool table with stacks of rumpled bills before them.

"Think this makes us even," Taurus said.

Quest muttered something foul while counting the bills he thumbed through. "I don't know about that. Your stash looks way healthier than mine."

"Hell man, don't you think I'm entitled?" Taurus grinned though his light eyes never veered from the *stash* he counted. "You've been whippin' my ass every day we've played."

"Sorry." Quest sent his cousin a guilty shrug. "Guess I should thank you for being here otherwise I'd have been on the phone naggin' Michaela. Quay stopped taking my calls a week ago." He referred to his wife and brother respectively.

Taurus chuckled, patting the back pockets of his jeans for his wallet. "Sounds like they're havin' fun whenever I talk to Nile." He spoke of his wife who; along with Michaela and the baby, had taken flight to California to visit the family Mick had just discovered.

"I thank God everyday she's found them," Quest shrugged again. "Doesn't mean I have to like her being gone so long."

"Hmph. Yeah…what's it been? Two days?"

"Go screw yourself." Quest's mouth twitched on a smirk. "And shut up, you're makin' me lose count."

A Lover's Shame

Soft laughter rose between the men until they were interrupted by the doorbell.

"Time for work?" Taurus asked, nodding toward the package his cousin had to sign for.

"Papers from Drake," Quest explained, referring to Drake Reinard- Chief Operating Officer at the Ramsey World offices in Sion, Switzerland.

"How's it goin' with the dismantling of the weapons division?" Taurus folded the bills into his wallet and watched Quest thumb through the bound report. "Everything still smooth with that?"

"Smooth as it'll get." Quest scanned the papers referring to that very topic.

"Right," Taurus closed his eyes resignedly. "You made a lot of people unhappy with this decision."

Quest's handsome molasses dark face seemed darker in the wake of sudden tension. "Unhappy is an understatement- especially since I've shut down one of Ramsey's biggest money makers." He waved the hefty report. "Info on every department affected by the dismantling- how many people are employed, how much money is being brought in and where it's going...purchase bids from other corporations- it's all here."

Taurus whistled and dragged a hand through the silky light brown waves of his hair. "Lotta people- lotta money."

"Yeah..." Quest tossed the report to an end table. "I owe a lot to Drake and his staff- they managed to find places for every displaced employee and at their current rate of pay."

Again, Taurus whistled. "Impressive."

"Especially these days," Quest folded his arms over the lightweight Hampton sweatshirt he wore and eyed the report. "I've got to go through that son of a bitch, sign off on the original and messenger it back to Drake in Sion."

"I don't envy you. But on a happy note," Taurus grinned. "It'll keep you busy until Mick and Quincee get back."

Quest rolled his eyes. "Busy yes. Entertained? No." He sighed and tilted his head toward the pool table. "You got time for another go?"

Taurus retrieved some of the new found stash from his wallet. "Rack 'em."

***

Sabella broke every speed limit on her way to Brogue's compound. Several times along the way, she tried reaching him on her phone. He wasn't answering. No surprise there.

When she arrived, he was outside waiting for her. Belle almost forgot to shut off the Lexus' ignition when she put the rental in park. Grabbing her bag, she scrambled out of the car. The heels of her bronze scrunch boots echoed against the stone drive as she raced toward Brogue.

"Is she here?" Belle was expectant and out of breath.

Brogue took pity. Stepping close, he smoothed his hands along the sleeves of the Dijon colored wrap dress that swung about her boots.

"Brogue?"

"Honey you should calm down."

"No. *You* should tell me about my mother." Her brilliant almond colored gaze searched his face.

"Honey I'm sorry," Brogue scratched at his temple. "I shouldn't have misled you but I wasn't sure you'd come if you knew I called you about Pike."

"Isak?" Belle's demeanor changed and she finally took notice of the black truck several feet from where she'd parked her car. Turning back to Brogue, she balled her hands against his chest. "Where is he?"

Brogue cupped a hand around her arm and took her inside.

"It's open," Brogue said to Belle when they stood before the chrome doors Pike had crashed through over an hour earlier.

Belle studied the door and then turned suspicious eyes on Brogue.

"We don't dare go in there." He admitted.

"Why? Who's in there?"

"Your uncle."

Realization dawned and Belle wasted not another minute. She pushed; with great effort, past the heavy doors. The smell almost knocked her back before she got one foot across the threshold. It warned her to turn back, that the smell was not the worst of what lay beyond. She closed her eyes hoping to ward off the scent of blood, shit and sweat. Emboldened somewhat, she moved into the room.

"Isak... Isak?" She spoke softly. There was no need to yell. The space was massive and cold. The walls were paneled with some sort of dark, metallic material. Her voice seemed to echo.

Her heels scraped the concrete floor. She stopped short of where a filmy sheen of... something she didn't want to identify, coated the area. The space was sparsely lit thanks to the one fluorescent light which appeared to be on its last circuit. Squinting through the unnerving flickering glow, she thought she saw the outline of a body lying several feet in front of her.

Before she could move closer to investigate, a hand folded over her arm. She screamed as her captor whirled her around to face him.

"Isak..." Her relief mixed with a considerable amount of unease. She took several deep breaths, bowing her head while resting her hands on his chest for support.

His face was shadowed by the weak lighting. Pike inhaled the scent of her. The provocative aroma cut through the foulness of the room. Before the sweetness could totally work its magic, he stiffened and gave her a rough jerk.

"What the hell are you doing here?" He bit out the question seconds before he answered it. "Brogue," he readjusted the grip on her arm intending to take her from the room.

A Lover's Shame

She braced against it. "Come with me."

"Later."

Digging her heels in, Belle bristled more firmly. "I won't leave without you." She knew he could see the horror in her eyes as she watched him. His clothes were splattered with blood or some other matter she didn't want to think about. His lush, blue black hair was in disarray, lying in a tumble over his head and into his deep gaze.

Swallowing down her emotions, Belle curved her fingers tightly into his shirt. "Please come with me."

"Bella…" Pike was torn between the anger ruling his head and the desire feeding his heart. "In a minute, alright?"

Sabella glanced toward the body on the floor and shook her head. "No."

Pike flexed his fingers about her arms as they kneaded the material of her dress. His eyes were focused on the floor.

Belle watched him at war with himself. Her courage was at its peak then.

"Belle-"

"No." She looked at her…uncle.

Pike grimaced and put himself between her and Marcus. "Soon," his tone left no room for argument.

Belle didn't care. "Isak…" She didn't know what had happened, but could make an accurate enough guess.

Marcus was groaning as he rolled over in his own blood and feces on the cold floor. If Pike didn't leave with her then, she feared the worst. Marc would say anything to get Pike to go including sharing a confession that he could never hear.

"Leave with me now," she tugged on his shirt with new intensity. "We can-we can have a drink and calm down. Isak please…"

Pike's expression changed then somehow. He watched Belle as though he'd found the last piece of a puzzle he'd been desperate to finish. "I don't want a drink." He said slowly.

"Alright- alright…" She sighed, her eyes still trained in the direction where Marc lay even though she couldn't see him around Pike. "That's fine. We can um… we can just go somewhere and talk."

He didn't move. "I don't want to talk."

Belle took her mind off Marcus and focused on Pike then. She couldn't see what was in his eyes. They were completely shadowed, given the poor lighting. His voice though…his voice told her exactly what she would need to offer to get him to leave.

"Just come with me Isak."

"Come with you and do what?"

She swallowed on the need his question roused inside her. "Whatever you want," she managed.

He curved his hand about her neck and forced her chin up with his thumb. "Do you understand what you're saying to me?" He moved his hand so she could nod.

"You understand that if you change your mind, I come back and finish this?"

A Lover's Shame

"I understand Isak." Once more she nodded. "I understand."

FIVE

"My car," Belle was about to accept Pike's help into the truck when she remembered the rental.

His grip tightened at her elbow and he cast a slight nod toward the Lexus.

"We'll take care of it."

Sabella looked back toward the rock encrusted entrance of the compound. She missed the way Pike's eyes wandered awe-struck across her hair. The wind had lifted a few tendrils from her French roll and had set them to waving about her face.

A Lover's Shame

"What's Marcus doing in there?" She asked him. Again, she felt his hold tighten.

"We'll talk about it." He promised, the sourness returning to his mood at her mention of the man.

Belle nodded, but the question was already dismissed. Instead, she'd become distracted by the way the breeze captured the fresh shirt Pike had borrowed from Brogue. He hadn't finished buttoning it and; as the crisp air wrestled with the fabric, it revealed a toned bronzed torso. His chest was a sleek wall of muscle void of hair and marked by only the brand signifying his fraternity.

She bit down on her lip, her teeth threatening to break the skin. Her fingers ached to see if he still felt like silk over steel. The sound of her name on his voice, broke into the fantasy.

Pike helped her settle into the truck. He stilled himself from going so far as to strap her into the seat. Instead, he shut the passenger door and went to meet Brogue who stood near the truck's flatbed.

Pike joined him there and pulled down the tailgate. Taking a seat there, he exchanged his soiled boots for a pair of sneakers also courtesy of his cousin.

"What'd you tell her?" He asked, while tossing the boots to the back of the truck.

"Only that Marc's here," Brogue folded his arms across his chest and briefly shifted his stare toward the front of the truck. "She's got no idea who put him here or why."

"Sure she does." Pike fixed Brogue with a deliberate smirk and watched him shrug.

"What the hell, I'm used to bein' the bad guy. Belle's an angel. She doesn't deserve to be drawn into this anymore than she has been."

"Why'd you call her?"

"You were goin' in there to kill the son of a bitch."

Pike focused on tying a sneaker. "I was goin' to question him." The argument sounded half-hearted.

"Did you get your answers?"

Pike offered no reply.

Brogue nodded. "*That's* why I called her. You would've killed the man. She's the only one who could've pulled you off."

"He's been here for months. Why hasn't Carmen killed him yet?" Pike dragged a hand through the windblown tufts of his hair. "I mean, I understand how gratifying torture can be but she's not even here to witness the bulk of it." He squeezed his eyes shut then, feeling the unexpected pressure of tears behind them. He pressed fingers to the bridge of his nose before those tears could appear.

"She's got every right to want him dead." Pike sounded as if he were speaking to himself then.

Curiosity lurked in Brogue's bright stare as he studied his cousin.

"Where is she? Carmen?" Pike asked suddenly.

Just as suddenly, Brogue diverted his gaze. Massaging his jaw, he looked toward the horizon. He knew

A Lover's Shame

Pike would break his neck in the time it'd take to blink. Sadly, for him death would be a welcomed choice against the tortures awaiting him should he confess what he knew of Carmen Ramsey's whereabouts.

"She makes contact through a cell-untraceable. The calls don't last very long." He lied, expelling a quiet sigh of relief when his cousin appeared to buy it.

"You tell me when she shows up here." Pike's words weren't delivered in the form of a request.

"You got it." Brogue looked toward the front of the truck again. "Where are you taking her?"

"Wherever it is, she'll be with me." Pike stood and slammed the tailgate back into place. "I won't let her out of my sight again."

"What happened with Marc, man?" Brogue was more than a little uneasy by then.

"You just call me if Carmen shows up here."

Nodding heartily, Brogue silently reconfirmed his promise to do so. "What do I tell her if she happens to ask about her daughter? I'm guessing it's safe to say you're not taking her back to meet the eight o'clock curtain for her play."

Pike's expression then was a mix of something both humorous and cunning. Brogue didn't know which set him more on edge.

Pike was on his way to the driver's side door when he stopped. "You tell my mother-in-law that the next time she sees her daughter, she better damn well be ready to tell her the truth."

***

San Sebastian Peninsula, Mozambique~

Carmen Ramsey stretched like a satisfied kitten. She felt especially warmed by the African sun beaming upon her back and by the man who held her secure against his dark body. Her contented stretching roused him from the light nap he was enjoying.

With a lazy smile curving his mouth, Jasper Stone leaned over and let his lips skim Carmen's shoulders. They were bared by the cut of her swimsuit. She turned in his arms and they indulged in a kiss as heated as the sun drenching their bodies.

Lovers once more; following their lengthy separation decades earlier, the couple had treasured a three year affair. Carmen had no idea that her decision to approach Brogue Tesano about helping her with Marcus would lead her back to her first love. Life though, was a funny thing.

Brogue had come to Carmen hoping to align himself with the powerful politicians for whom she arranged campaign fundraisers. Aware of his background; thanks to her daughter, Carmen acted on a whim and approached the dangerous Tesano about taking down her brother.

Little did Carmen know that the plan was already in the works. Jasper's connection to the Tesano family hadn't been nearly as stunning as the discovery of what he'd done with his life. Carmen had at first been unaware of how powerful Jasper had become in his field. How powerful he'd become soon became obvious in light of the lavish trips and gifts he'd showered when Brogue brought her to his door.

A month after they'd reunited; Jasper lavished Carmen with another gift- an engagement ring. It was a gift she'd refused. He never asked again but promised they'd revisit the topic once he'd extinguished all her demons- demons she had yet to fully discuss with him. Regardless, the slow destruction of Marcus Ramsey made the time pass quite nicely.

"When are you leaving me?" Jasper asked once their kiss ended.

She fixed him with a playfully hurt expression. "That ready to be rid of me, huh?"

He wasn't amused. "I never want you away from me again but it won't happen until that jackass is in the ground."

Carmen's expression changed while she smoothed her hand down his cheek.

"What?" He brushed fingers across the furrow in her brow. "Are you having second thoughts?"

"Never." Her response was lightning fast and sincerity sparkled in her light eyes. "Brogue tells me the idiot's losing his fight."

"Does Brogue think he'll die before we kill him?"

"I don't know…" Carmen focused on the silky line of hair snaking down Jasper's still muscular abdomen. "But however he goes, I want to be there to see it."

Jasper's very attractive features appeared to tighten. "I expect this next trip to be your last. I want it done this time."

Carmen swallowed with effort, though she couldn't argue with his command. It was past time. *Way* past time.

"You should probably come with me if it's about to end, then."

Jasper tensed. Talk of visiting the States was not his favorite subject, not even for the chance to witness Marc Ramsey's demise.

They were interrupted then by one of the house staff asking if they'd take drinks outside before dinner.

"Do you need me there?" He asked once they were alone again. After all the years that had passed between them, he'd still walk through fire for her.

Carmen kissed his jaw and then leaned back to search his face intensely. "I *want* you there." She whispered just as intensely and then shuddered when he drew her close.

Yes, she wanted him there. Before that could happen though, she'd have to confide what she'd kept hidden for over three decades. She'd have to tell the man she loved why she'd turned away from what they could've had.

***

Sabella opened the door but stood just inside the suite and watched as Pike followed. She kept swallowing around the lumps of emotion that threatened to stifle her breathing. Her stomach was a rolling mass of nerves. She felt more unsteady than she had the first night they made love.

The thought of so long ago caused her to moan. Thankfully, Pike was too busy checking the suite to overhear her. When he returned to the front, what he said wasn't what she expected at all.

"Get packed. I'm going to my room for a shower, then we're out."

Belle could feel her mouth curve into a perfect O. She didn't think to wonder if he'd noticed her surprise (or disappointment).

"You'll probably want to check in with Martin and Arthur. Tell 'em something so they won't be worried."

She propped a hand to her hip. "What do you suggest I tell them when I don't even know where we're going?"

Pike's gaze sharpened in response to her challenge and he moved closer. "Does where we're going, matter?"

"It matters. It matters to me."

He cast his black stare toward the floor. "Are you afraid to be alone with me, Bella?"

"No…" her voice was a whisper, floating on another moan. "It's only…"

"Are you going back on our agreement?" His eyes were focused on hers that time.

She could barely shake her head.

In spite of it all, Pike felt the urge to smile. The world could be raging and her closeness could settle it all for him. Instinctively, he made a move to touch her, but resisted. He couldn't do it, not with the stench of that devil still clinging to him.

He treated himself to a simple kiss which he placed lightly at her temple.

"I'll be back in a couple of hours," he promised focusing on a wavy tendril of her hair clinging to his thumb. He left her then with an easy wink and smile.

Outside her room door, he dropped the façade. He bowed his head and braced a fist on either side of the door. The tears he'd felt; pressing behind his eyes at the compound, stirred again. He refused the urge to give into them and headed on down the hall.

Inside her room, Belle questioned the change in events. She'd been anticipating what would happen once they got wherever they were going. Being brought back to her hotel and told to pack, had her confused to say the very least.

Then there was the most confusing thing of all. Marc's presence in Brogue Tesano's... chamber. Belle paced the living area and debated over whom to call. She hadn't been told to keep Marc's captivity a secret, but why was he there? Why had Brogue called her there to pull Isak off him and why was Isak there trying to beat him to death?

Maybe he knows, the whisper inside her head was brief. She shrugged. Who *wouldn't* want to beat Marcus Ramsey to death? The man had been pretty much an enigma to her while growing up. She never spent any time alone with him and rarely in the presence of others.

A Lover's Shame

She'd come to know her cousins Moses, Fernando and Yohan outside the presence of their father. Her mother had never talked about him...understandably. Belle had never questioned it. Marcus Ramsey hadn't been a factor in her life at all. Then; in the irony that life seemed to thrive upon, she'd discovered he'd been the biggest factor of all.

It was then that Belle noticed her hands were shaking. She could actually feel them trembling- a sure sign that she'd gone too long without her meds. Clenching and unclenching her hands, she went to the bedroom where the pill bottle waited on the dresser. Without hesitation, she cracked into the bottle; swallowed one of the small oval capsules and chased it with water from the half-filled glass next to her perfume.

She leaned against the dresser while everything washed down. Afterwards, she reached for the bottle; turning it over in a now steady hand.

Panic attacks. She smirked, thinking of the nasty side-affect to her discovery of her mother and Marc. At least the pills had helped her slim down- *some* as her ex-husband had detected. Actually, it was the walking away from Isak that started the attacks.

Now, there he was again having arrived as smoothly and as unexpectedly as he'd done the first time she'd met him.

Belle shook off those thoughts and decided packing her things would go a long way in quieting long ago memories. The light was flashing on the room phone. She had an idea of who it was before she even listened to the message.

Martin called to check on her since she'd missed morning rehearsals. She set down her phone and proceeded to shoving things into her bags. She'd have to tell them something.

She'd have to tell them the truth. Martin and Arthur had been so good to her. They deserved the truth.

And what about Isak? Didn't he deserve the truth? That he did went without saying. But how was she to tell him, when just the thought of it made her sick inside.

Following a long, blisteringly hot shower, Pike sat rubbing a towel through his wet hair as he spoke with his father over the phone.

"Beats the hell out of me," Roman Tesano was saying to his second oldest son. "I have no idea who in the family would sic Brogue on Marcus and the fact that his own sister approached Brogue with it…hell that's just *too* strange."

"Could you believe that maybe he just decided to help her, dad?"

Brogue?" Roman's hearty laughter flooded the line mere seconds after he'd uttered his nephew's name.

"It could happen." Pike mused after he'd join his father in a moment of much needed laughter. "Brogue knows Carmen's my mother-in-law…ex…"

"How's Belle?" Roman asked after silence held the line for half a minute.

"She…" Pike wound the towel about his wrist. "She's as beautiful as she ever was, Dad. She still loves me."

"Pike…"

"She still loves me, Dad. I know it. I know she does."

"Alright son, alright."

"Can't you see it, Dad? I mean, can't you see it when Mama looks at you? Don't you just know it when she looks at you?"

"I do. Hell yes, I do. But we're not talking about your mother and me. You be careful with that girl. Whatever it was that made her walk away from you- she may not be ready to deal with it even if it means coming back to you."

Pike nodded, his gaze fixed on the damp towel he twirled about his arm. Calling home had been the right move. Next to Belle, his parents were the only ones who could still the rage when it took hold.

"So tell me, did *you* believe your cousin when he told you his father hadn't sent him after Ramsey?"

Pike was thankful for the subject change. "I believed him. Whoever it is, they're bad enough to have Brogue scared witless."

"Hmph. That ain't an easy thing to do. At any rate, I can't say that I've heard any rumbles about Brogue aside from him being responsible for Yvonne Wilson's death."

"Yvonne and Houston and Daphne Ramsey."

Pike's additional information sent another stream of silence through the phone line.

"Jesus…" Roman breathed. "Brogue told you this?"

"Mmm hmm," Pike tossed the towel to the coffee table. "What are you thinkin', Dad?"

"That something's going on behind the family's back."

"And Brogue's dead in the middle of it."

SIX

"I *told* you." Arthur said while snapping fingers toward his partner.

Sabella's long almond stare shifted between her friends. "Will you make me guess?" She asked when Arthur didn't appear to be of a mind to explain himself.

Arthur's shrug sent the sequins glittering on his money green shirt. "I told Martin that I figured you'd slept together."

Belle's mouth fell open. "The other night?" She straightened and turned to face Arthur more fully on the sofa they shared.

"Oh stop it," he waved a hand about his head. "There was barely any room between the two of you on the dance floor that night."

Because it'd do her good and because she couldn't stifle it, Belle laughed. Martin and Arthur shared patient smiles and waited.

"I didn't sleep with Isak Tesano that night." She said once she'd composed herself.

Martin helped himself to another shot of Tequila. "Must've been the next night, then."

That time, Belle doubled over when she laughed.

Arthur refused to let his colleague off the hook. "The man had every woman in the cast drooling."

"Hell, he had every *man* in the cast drooling." Martin corrected before downing his shot.

Arthur pointed a finger in Martin's direction as though the man had just spoken the absolute truth. "No way are *you* immune." He told Sabella.

"No…" Her expression softened. "No I'm not immune. Nowhere near it," she smoothed her hands over the folds of her dress and smiled. "I slept with Isak Tesano about seven years ago."

Martin and Arthur were completely silent and completely stunned.

Belle figured she'd better seize the quiet while it lasted. "We were married and… things ended badly-"

A Lover's Shame

"You still love each other."

She flopped back on the couch.

"Don't even try denying it. His eyes were on you the minute you walked into the pub." Martin smirked as he remembered. "Whatever he was saying at the time, silenced quick."

"And you weren't any better." Arthur leaned over to tapped Belle's knee. "Actin' like you were about to melt every time you looked at him."

Belle left the sofa and began to pace the living area. Martin and Arthur exchanged concerned glances when they noticed the intensity in the way she wrung her hands.

"Honey? Are the two of you gonna try and make a go of it again?"

Belle sent Arthur a sad smile. "We're not even *close* to that. Too much has happened-*still* happening."

Martin made a pretense at straightening his red tie then walked over to where Belle stood near the work desk. "The only thing that matters is what's *happening* between the two of you right now."

Belle gave a half-hearted tug to the knot on Martin's tie. "What's *happening* is a mess all its own."

"So start with cleaning it up, then." Arthur advised from his spot on the sofa.

"And what happens if cleaning it up only creates another mess?"

"Belle…" Martin shook his head and moved close to kiss her cheek. "Then you clean that up too. Haven't you realized by now that relationships are just a series of messes needing to be cleaned up?"

"Then what's the point?" She laughed.

"The point rests in *why* you're willing to clean it up." Martin squeezed her upper arms. "Focus on the *why* of it and you'll find the messes won't always seem quite so messy."

Belle toyed with a lock of her hair and fixed her friends with a look of playful skepticism. "Do you two have an advice column somewhere that I don't know about?"

Martin burst into laughter as bowed his head. "No sweet, we've just been involved in a helluva lot of messes that we weren't willin' to stick around and clean up." He added.

Arthur came close to bump her shoulder with his. "Guess we could never lock in on the *why* of it."

"Listen, we're gonna give you some space, alright?" Martin moved to his toes and placed a kiss to Belle's jaw. "We'll explain everything to the gang. You just need to keep in touch- let us know you're okay."

"'Kay," Belle nodded quickly and pulled them into hugs before they could see the tears glistening in her eyes.

Martin and Arthur left soon after. Belle guessed she had just enough time to shower and change before heading out to parts unknown with Pike. She undressed and was on her way to the bathroom when the bell rang.

A Lover's Shame

Arthur and Martin. One of them was always forgetting something. She shimmied into a long chenille robe as the bell sounded again.

"Coming!" She laughed, trying to slip a few tendrils back into her loose French roll.

"What'd you forget?" She asked, while pulling open the door.

"This," Pike responded a split second before his mouth was crushing hers.

No thought of resistance or hesitation came to Belle's mind. She quite literally melted against him eager to play an equal part in the sudden battle their tongues fought against the forceful kiss.

Pike moved past the door, kicking it shut with the heel of a tanned suede hiking boot. He kept one hand curved about her throat, while the other fisted into the robe's soft fabric and gathered it at her hip.

Belle's hands weren't still either. Greedy to feel every part of him, she glided her fingers through the thick waves of his still damp hair. Her French-tipped nails raked the cottony soft whiskers shadowing his face, down the chords flexing along his neck and then onto his chest hidden beneath the Giants sweatshirt he wore outside sagging light blue denims.

She wasn't frightened by the low, ragged sounds churning deep inside his throat as his tongue searched every crevice of her mouth. She met the savagery of the kiss with a fierceness of her own. Her heart beat double time in her ears, a response to the hushed manner he spoke her name in the midst of his making love to her mouth.

Pike leaned back on the door and ground her into his arousal. A shuddery groan roused full and hungry past her lips as she moved erotically- *shamelessly* against the very satisfying bulge below his waist.

Belle's robe was gradually losing its fight to cling to her body. Pike was tugging it from her back while changing the tilt of his head as they kissed.

Belle's moans turned into a whimper when Pike unexpectedly broke the kiss.

"No..." she stood on her toes, hungry for it to continue.

Pike wanted her out of the robe. He drew it away in a final quick tug that revealed her to his seductive black stare. What Sabella saw lurking in the bottomless orbs, threatened to stop the throbbing of her heart.

A hint of wariness struck her then as she stood there before him with no shields- no barriers. Her sparkling stare faltered and then she would have made a move to cover some part of herself.

Pike stopped her before she could do so. His hand curved about her neck once again. He used his thumb to nudge her chin, tilting it up and back and forcing her to meet his gaze. He kissed her again, outlining the ridge of her teeth before enticing her tongue to play with his.

Belle shivered that time; not from cold, but from his strong fingers playing their sensual tune upon her skin.

A Lover's Shame

Torturing her yet again, he ended the kiss and she retaliated by beating her fist once against the brick that was his chest.

The pecan brown of her skin beckoned his mouth to taste. God, he'd missed her! His perfectly crafted lips explored the line of her neck, sampling the undeniable sweetness that lay within the richness of her complexion. Her natural fragrance combined with the perfume she wore, had him intoxicated and out of his mind for her.

He dipped his head to ravish more of her body with open mouthed kisses. Belle nuzzled her face into the crook of his neck. She'd become just as intoxicated and out of her mind for him. Hungrily, she nibbled his earlobe, suckling his flesh and then soothing it with her tongue. Perfect teeth bit down gently into her shoulder as he cradled the enticing fullness of her breasts in his palms.

"Isak…" she whispered, arching herself, offering herself. All the while she prayed he'd do more than just hold her there.

He must have heard her silent plea. His thumbs applied a dual caress to her nipples. She sobbed at the exquisite pleasure the simple touch ignited.

"Isak, mmm…"

"Tell me," he urged, leaning back to study her lovely dark face and the affect he had on her. "Tell me what you want me to do."

"Put your mouth on me, Isak please…"

"Where?"

"Everywhere."

Her response sent the strength from his legs. In one move, he took her down with him to the floor. Belle shivered; again not from the cold, but from the decadent feel of his hair falling across her chest like the brush of a silk scarf.

Languidly, she pulled her fingers through the onyx waves and cried out when his tongue encircled a nipple before drawing it into his mouth. The friction of his clothes against her bare skin was as much a stimulant as the mink texture of his beard.

Pike made his way down her body, leaving no part of her unattended. Whatever concerns that may have lingered for Belle; regarding her appeal to him, vanished in that moment. His soft chanting of her name as he nuzzled his face into her belly and lower, set her on fire with confidence in her allure and beauty.

He'd always made her feel as though he saw no one else but her. He hadn't lost that ability. She was desperate for him then to be as naked as she, to view the beautiful copper tone of his body, to welcome him inside her love.

Pike was at the limit of his restraint, but couldn't seem to tear himself away from the taste and smell of her. The closer he ventured to the part of her he most yearned for, the more ravenous he felt. Her miniscule cries; as he tended to some new place on her body, stroked his ego to a frenzied state.

He was ravenous indeed by the time he'd settled between the lush expanse of her thighs. For a time, he simply took in her scent unrivaled by any man-made fragrances. He spread her so that he could feast to his content.

Belle pressed her head into the plush carpeting. Meanwhile, she raised her hips eager to meet the erotic lunges and rotations of his tongue.

Pike rested his hands to the tops of her thighs to keep her in place. Immobile and being pleasured to the point of madness, Belle rolled her head back and forth while being claimed by a powerful orgasmic wave.

Pike chose to watch the emotions take over her lovely features as she climaxed. Her lashes were fluttering open as he moved up over her. That time, it was Pike claimed by the force of emotion as he witnessed the love in her eyes.

Wantonly, Belle raised her head to ply him with a kiss. As though starved, she curved her tongue over and under his obsessed with drinking the taste of her body from his mouth.

Pike rose up over her suddenly and Belle bit down on her lip. Her vivid gaze sparkled with anticipation as he whipped the sweatshirt over his head.

Awestruck, she reached out to stroke the bronzed plane of his magnificent torso cut with an array of muscles that flexed against every move he made. She halted briefly to outline the horseshoe brand that stretched when he breathed.

She reached for the fly of his jeans and worked to undo the buttons straining against a considerable erection.

Pike grunted, succumbing to the pleasure that the simple act instilled. He hunched over her, bracing on his fists which accentuated the chords in his forearms.

Belle's eyes narrowed as she worked with the button fly. She practically sizzled over the expectancy of what lay beneath it and let out a sound of elation and need when his impressive length was freed.

Pike covered her again as she guided his body inside hers. A heavy shudder overwhelmed him when the tip of his sex nudged hers. With no small effort, he raised his head. He wanted to look into her eyes as he took her.

"See me," he urged when she would have closed her eyes. He waited until she complied before continuing his journey inside her.

Again, Pike felt his ego freshly stroked by the helpless sounds rising from her throat. She was incredibly tight and; while the feeling promised to stop his heart, he pressed onward. His own helpless sounds mingled with hers.

Belle was trembling terribly. She was clearly overwrought by sensations she never dared hope she'd feel again. She would have locked her legs about his back, but he kept them apart deepening his penetration and heightening their enjoyment.

She covered his hands where they rested on her thighs, squeezing their suppleness while his thrusts forced a wealth of moisture from her center.

"Bella...God..." he groaned, kissing her again as his seed spilled deep a long while later. His thrusts lost

A Lover's Shame

none of their intensity. He wasn't ready to end it yet. She began to clench her inner walls about him and his hands grew too weak to support the hold on her thighs.

Triumphant then, Belle locked her legs about his waist and took whatever he had left to give.

"Belle please…" he collapsed upon her then spent and satisfied.

Pressing a hard kiss to the top of his head, Belle nuzzled her face into his hair and then gave into her own exhaustion.

SEVEN

Pike was the first to awaken from the deep sleep he and Belle had fallen into after they'd made love again and again. And they had *made love*. Despite the spontaneity and desperation of the act, the love fueled it all. It was practically tangible, almost seen.

Pike showered again, dressed without waking her and then sat on the bed to watch her sleep. She rested on her stomach, her hair splayed in a tumble of chestnut brown ribbons across the pillows.

A Lover's Shame

He watched, mesmerized not only by her appeal but by who she was- who she *still* was. After all those horrible years, she still possessed every part of his heart.

She snuggled one side of her face deeper into the pillow she clutched and uttered a subconscious sigh of relaxation. Pike had to smile, enjoying the sight of her so content, so secure. The anger, which always loomed close to the surface, took hold again inside him. This time, it didn't manifest in a need to punish but to protect.

Through no fault of her own, the woman he loved had been thrown into a terrible mess created by others. She had faced her storm alone and unable to trust anyone with the secret she carried. Did she really think he could stop loving her because of it? Did she really think being the product of such brutality made her any less worthy? Did she expect him to believe she was any less incredible?

He smoothed a hand lightly down her bare back and focused on the flawless rich brown of her skin. Slowly his fingers trailed downward until they touched the sheet twisted about her lower half.

Possession filtered the dark of his eyes as they followed the line of his touch. His smile was one of pure male appreciation as he observed the rise of her ample bottom beneath the sheet. He treated himself to a few soft squeezes and grunted when she shifted beneath the covers which caused her derriere to nudge his palm and fill it.

She'd yet to awaken and Pike felt it best to leave her alone before he climbed back into bed with her. They had time before having to leave. It was better to let her get her rest. She was going to need it.

With that in mind, he stood and tucked in the covers around her. He leaned close to brush a kiss to her temple and lingered a bit longer to inhale the hint of perfume clinging to the crook of her neck. He was making his way out of the bedroom, when his path shifted toward the dresser.

The pill bottle had drawn his attention. Curious, Pike reached for it, weighing it against his palm. He looked back toward Sabella and then turned back to scan the prescription.

"Doctor Ewan Breneman," he whispered, "once a day with meal…" Again, he weighed the bottle in his hand before returning it to where it'd sat on the dresser.

Pike left the bedroom, pulling the phone from his jeans as he shut the door. His party answered after two rings. Soon he was greeting his frat brother in their usual manner and laughing when Quest Ramsey responded in turn.

"How's it goin'?" Quest bellowed. He was as happy to hear from his frat as he was for an excuse to take a break from going through the monstrous report littering his desk.

"Good." Pike walked the perimeter of the living area and decided not to waste time getting to the point of his call. "Belle's with me."

Of course nothing had prepared Quest for that bit of information. He tried, with great determination to voice an adequate reply. "Huh?" Was all he could manage.

A Lover's Shame

Pike took pity on the man's confusion and gave him a truly condensed version of how his foundation had given money to Belle's play.

"Right," Quest's monotone spoke volumes. Clearly he wasn't fooled. "So you guys just *happened* to decide on that play?" He reared back in his desk chair and took pleasure in grilling his friend. "Out of all the others in the world, this one needed help the most?"

"I've been having her followed."

"For how long?"

"Oh…" Pike hesitated to stare out at Portland's early evening skies for a moment. "About two years after she divorced me. About the time I stopped feelin' sorry for myself and decided to do something about it."

"Uh huh…and torturing yourself by having her followed was the best way to *do* something about it?"

"She still loves me, Q."

Quest sent a barely muffled groan through the line.

"It's true. She didn't walk away from me because she wanted to."

Quest straightened in his chair. "Is she alright? Has anybody-?"

"No, no Q. It's not what you think." Pike took a heavy breath and commenced to pacing the room again.

"So what is it, then?" Quest didn't bother to disguise the tightness in his voice. "Pike?"

"I can't go into it- it's complicated Q."

"What the hell does that mean?"

"That means it's between Bella and me. I need you
to trust me here, man."

Quest took time with his response. His protective
streak where Belle, Sabra and Sybilla were concerned was
almost as intense as the one he carried for Michaela.

"Please Q?" Pike urged, understanding the man's
reluctance.

"Alright," the reply sounded halfhearted. Quest put
a little more effort into it. "Alright. So where is she now?"

"She's with me." Pike looked toward the bedroom
door. "I plan on keepin' it that way. I only called in case
anybody got worried."

Quest grinned and swiveled his chair to and fro.
"Anybody being my cousins?"

"Especially the fine ones," Pike clarified.

"Hmph. More especially- Sabra," Quest chuckled as
she came to mind. "Alright then. You can count on me so
long as Belle keeps close to her phone."

"She'll have it all the time." Pike rested a hand to
his chest as he gave his word. "I promise I'll bring her
home the second she asks me."

"Liar," Quest accused in a playful voice. "You be
easy with her, man." There was no hint of the playful in his
tone then.

Pike nodded. "I swear it, Q." Again he looked
toward the closed bedroom door. "She's gone through hell
and dealt with too much of it on her own. I can't abide by
that- not anymore. Can you understand what I mean?"

A Lover's Shame

Quest had already taken Mick's picture from the corner of his desk. "Yeah man," he brushed his fingers across her face smiling out at him, "Damn right I can."

***

Harlem, New York~

"Are you sure there's nothing else I can do to make you more comfortable, Mr. Tesano?"

Roman smiled and set aside the three month old issue of *Car and Driver*. "I'm fine, sweetheart. Don't go troubling yourself."

Alana Raymond's slightly slanting stare sparkled a bit more behind the stylish frames perched on her nose. "It's definitely no trouble Mr. Tesano."

"I didn't think about how busy your boss was before I dropped in to chat without an appointment." Roman told the young woman.

Alana settled to the arm of the sofa Roman occupied. "You know you never need an appointment to drop by," she leaned over to prop her elbow to the back of the sofa. Her silk mosaic print blouse was unbuttoned to the rise of her breasts. She kept her eyes trained on Roman's while her fingers grazed the dark caramel toned skin visible just above her bra. "You promise to let me know if there's anything at all I can do to make your wait more enjoyable?"

Flattered; yet far from tempted, Roman let his impossibly long lashes shield his stare for an exaggerated moment. "I'm fine Alana but," he gave a final push to the magazine and stood, "I probably should get going."

"Oh." Alana blinked and straightened from her Mata Hari recline on the sofa. She slid from the arm and followed her boss's brother as he made his way toward the front of the decadent penthouse office overlooking Uptown.

Roman's steps halted suddenly. Alana stumbled to a stop on her six inch heels so as not to slam into his back. A baritone voice roared from the corridor as its owner drew near.

"We're gonna wait, I said. The muthafucka's gonna fold, I can feel it." Pitch Tesano bolted through the double oak doors of the office. His phone in one hand, the other pressed to the ear piece where he took the call. His thumb worked impressively over the keypad as he texted. It took him almost a minute to realize his younger brother was there and smiling at him from just a few feet away.

It took less than a second for Pitch to end the call and cease the texting. "Little brother!" he greeted the man who stood as tall; though not as broad, as he did. Laughing, he tugged Roman into a tight hug and kissed his cheek. Pitch was a gregarious sort who could instill humor as quickly as fear.

"This is a good surprise!" He squeezed Roman's shoulder just as his dark olive-tone face tensed with concern. "Is Immi alright?"

Roman smiled as his wife's image flooded his mind. "She's fine."

A Lover's Shame

Pitch nudged his brother's arm with a beefy fist. "She ready to leave you for me, yet?"

"Not a chance."

"Only a matter of time, Rome..." Pitch sang in a playfully foreboding manner.

"So you've been saying for the last thirty some odd years." Roman sighed, dropping an arm around his brother's shoulders as they headed back into the office.

"So what brings you Uptown?" Pitch tossed his phone and other gadgets to a monstrously large pine desk near the windows lining the rear of the room.

Roman's deep-set gaze shifted toward Alana who now perched along the window sill. "Got a minute to talk?" He asked his brother.

Pitch followed his brother's gaze toward the young woman. "'Lana baby, hold my calls alright?"

Alana bounced toward the door leading to an outer office but she stopped near her boss's desk. "Can I bring you two anything? Or have anything sent up?"

"Just hold my calls, honey." Pitch instructed softly then bumped her chin with his fist and sent her off with a wink.

Roman shook his head once they were alone. "Why don't you just put the girl out of her misery and sleep with her?"

Pitch chuckled. "Not too subtle, is she?" He smoothed a hand across the wavy crop of hair combed back from his strong deep copper-toned face. "Lana's just 'fillin in until Shelly gets back from vacation." He sighed, thinking of his executive assistant for the past twenty-two years. "Damn, I never knew I could miss that woman so much." He shrugged from the tailored jacket he wore. "Guess she really does deserve that raise she's been hinting about."

Roman hiked his tanned trousers and took a seat in the overstuffed arm chair before the desk. "So who's the kid?"

"Daughter of a friend."

"Ah…" Roman's dark eyes flashed with sudden understanding. "Which explains why you haven't taken her to bed yet."

"I swear I'm innocent." Pitch placed a hand over his heart and the other in the air. "Plus I'm not low down enough to sleep with the kid when her mother still warms my sheets."

"Muthafucka," Roman fell into laughter. "I swear you won't ever change!"

Pitch raised a shoulder, conceding the fact. "Hell, Candace would kill me if I ever looked Alana's way. Which I'd never do. I changed the girl's diapers for Chrissakes!"

"Candace?" Roman massaged his goatee and the square curve of his jaw while focusing on the name. "That Candace Strong's kid? I didn't know you had a thing with her?"

Again, Pitch shrugged while settling into a worn suede chair that looked out of place in the plush office. "We've always been off and on."

Roman leaned over and rested his elbows to his knees. "Were you two *on* when Alana came into the picture?"

"No. No Rome," Some of Pitch's good humor was starting to wear thin. "I guess in a perfect world Alana would've been mine- all mine and Candace would've damn well brought more than one kid into the world."

In spite of his brother's bravado, Roman could sense the true regret in his words. Candace Strong was black. She knew Pitch at a time when such attraction was as forbidden as it was life threatening. Roman understood the man's use of the phrase 'a perfect world'.

"Hell," Pitch grumbled and pushed back from the desk. It took some time for his thoughts (regrets) to return to their usual place at the back of his mind. Once they were tucked away, he fixed Roman with a suspicious glare. "Why'd you come see me today, Rome?"

"What do you know about the houseguest our nephew has at his place of business?"

"Brogue," Pitch massaged his temples knowing the rest of the story wouldn't be pleasant. "Guess we're gonna need drinks." He headed for the wall bar. "Who's the guest?" He asked over his shoulder.

"A Ramsey."

Pitch stilled his stride.

"Marcus." Roman decided to keep the information flowing and told his brother everything he knew including how Brogue played into the deaths of Houston and Daphne Ramsey.

"How do you know all this?" Pitch was bracing a hand to the edge of the bar for support.

"Pike."

"And *he* knows how?"

"Brogue told him."

"Just like that?"

Roman's smile was bittersweet. "My son's grown... more persuasive than he used to be."

"Ha!' Pitch went to prepare the drinks. "That's a fuckin' understatement!" He knew all too well about the young man's drastic personality change. "Did Brogue tell him who gave the order for it?"

"Brogue says it was no one in the family and brace yourself- Pike believed him."

Pitch whistled over the last tidbit and poured two glasses of Courvoisier. "Did he share any insights with Pike over *who* may have hired him?"

"He did more than share insights," Roman accepted the drink his brother offered. "He says he was hired by Carmen Ramsey." Roman set aside his drink lest he risk spilling it when he joined Pitch in roaring laughter.

"Carmen Ramsey?" Pitch downed his drink and then wiped the back of his hand across his mouth. "West's little sister Carmen?" He referred to their old friend and business partner Westin Ramsey.

"Same one," Roman sipped his drink.

"Damn...talk about a sweet piece..." Pitch shook his head as though he were envisioning the woman then. "What the fuck, Rome?"

A Lover's Shame

"Beats me," Roman braced an elbow to the arm of the chair and rested his chin in his palm.

"And I'm guessin' the rest of the Ramseys don't have a clue either?" Pitch poured another drink but nursed it instead of tossing it straight down. "Shit Rome, this is Brogue we're talkin' about. I don't care how good Carmen Ramsey looks or how many tears she shed no way is he gonna get tangled up in Ramsey family business like that."

"Someone backing her? Someone outside the family maybe?" Roman pondered.

"It's a stretch. Brogue's a wild man but he's loyal to that side of the family." Pitch decided to finish off the drink that time. "I can't see him jumpin' through hoops for someone outside of it."

"Unless he's afraid of 'em."

Pitch's laugh was a soft grunt. "We talkin' about the same bad ass nephew?"

"Pike said the boy looked scared. At the risk of a possible ass whippin' from Pike, he still wouldn't say a whole helluva lot about whom; if anyone, was backing Carmen."

"So that makes three things we need to find out." Pitch leaned over the bar. "Who-*if anyone*- is backing the lovely Ms. Ramsey. *Why* are they backing her and *why* the hell is our Brogue scared shitless?"

***

Deep in thought, Belle stood absently drying her hair. The edge of the bath sheet practically dragged the tile floor as it hung against her nude body still glistening from the shower. When she heard Pike clear his throat, she wrapped into the towel and observed him with a wary stare.

Pike braced off the jamb and came to her. Taking her wrist, he led her over to the counter and leaned against it. Belle's death grip on the towel slackened the second he touched her. She whimpered moments before his mouth fell on hers. Her fingers funneled through his gorgeous hair, rubbing his scalp and winding throughout the onyx mass that framed his devastating face.

Pike had done away with the towel preferring his hands cover her body instead. He cupped her butt, squeezing the lush cheeks while he lifted her into him.

Belle moaned helpless against the sensations rioting through her. She wasn't ashamed to bend to their will. Desperate for some friction to ease the bothersome tingles radiating from her nipples, she rubbed her breasts against the sweatshirt he wore. She caressed his tongue with hers, linking her arms about his neck while arching her bosom higher against his chest.

Pike's groan mixed with a more tortured sound. He'd only come to check on her. Now he could think of nothing except being inside her again. Her infrequent moaning as she rubbed against him and suckled his bottom lip had him breathless and too...well...*weak in the knees* to support himself.

Belle ended the kiss to trail another across Pike's whiskered jaw and down his neck. Hungry for the sight and taste of his chest, she tugged the hem of the shirt he wore.

Pushing up the fabric with feverish intensity, she kissed every patch of bronzed skin revealed to her.

"Belle…" He tried to resist- they had a schedule to keep. He cursed instead when she found one of his nipples and suckled there while moaning her pleasure.

"Honey wait," long lashes fluttered down over his eyes as he fought to keep his train of thought. "We gotta be goin' soon… Belle?"

"Mmm hmm?" Her fingers curved into the waistband of his jeans.

His powerful grip kneaded her bottom. "Wait… shit…wait…"

"Mmm mmm," she refused, still moaning while she fed on him.

Pike gave in to what she stirred. He lost his fingers in her hair, treasuring the heavy silkiness of it. A sharp stake of desire sent his erection to throbbing with greater intensity. Exhibiting remarkable willpower, he tried to pull her away.

"Stop," she whispered, yet drew away from his chest to begin a fresh assault on his earlobe.

"Baby, we gotta be goin'," he knew they'd never leave if he gave in.

"You really don't want this, now?" She spoke close to his ear and curved a hand over his inner thigh.

The thick ridge of his shaft lay stiff and aching. Pike muttered a curse and gave in to more kissing once he'd clutched her neck and guided her mouth back to his.

Belle laughed in the midst of the gesture. She was energized by all the missed pleasures her husband (ex) could bring to life with the simplest acts. Again, she squeezed the erection beneath his jeans.

Pike dug deep for just a shred of resistance and latched on when he found it. "We honestly have to get ready to go," he said. He wanted the traveling over and done with. Then she was all his.

Of course, Belle was in no hurry. She stood on her toes and suckled his ear while moving to undo his belt.

"Bella?" He cupped her round face and gave it the faintest tug. "No." His heart turned over when her generous well-kissed mouth curved into a pout. He honestly didn't see himself letting her out of bed at all during the first leg of their trip.

"I'll make it up to you." It was his turn to nuzzle her ear then. "Promise," He added and lightly gnawed her neck before giving her butt a final squeeze. "Goin' to get my stuff and change. Be ready in twenty." He ordered and left her to catch her breath and do as he'd asked.

EIGHT

Outside Kelowna, British Columbia~

"Impressed?" Pike asked once he'd rounded the side of the helicopter and was helping Belle from her seat.

"Where would you like for me to start?" She watched him in disbelief. "When'd you learn to fly? Or did you always have this up your sleeve?" She asked once she stood next to him outside the black and green striped chopper.

Pike smiled bashfully, his lashes shielding his stare as he focused on pulling off his gloves. "I got certified a few years back. Guess I tried some of everything to get you off my mind."

Belle was next to hide her eyes from view when she too looked elsewhere. She offered a quick prayer that nothing would spoil the magic of the last several hours. It had been too perfect and too missed to end...ever.

"This is incredible," she nodded towards the dwelling set quiet and majestic in a sea of green. The array of mountains far behind provided an overwhelming backdrop. "Is this new?" She referred to the grand cabin which sat a quarter mile beyond the helipad.

Pike was already slipping the straps of their bags over his shoulders. "The place has been in my family ever since my dad and uncles visited the Pacific Northwest back in the sixties." He secured the helicopter then took a moment to observe the vivid environment. "They each got equal shares from my granddad to buy the property and build the place."

They walked towards the house as Pike reminisced about times spent in such an elaborate setting.

"Me and Hill used to love comin' out here." Pike grinned thinking of his older brother Hilliam.

Belle looked up and all around. Her eyes were wide and as wonder-filled as a child's. "You and your brothers must've had some time running around in all this as little boys." The place looked drenched in green and appeared to float as one expanse of hillside rolled into another.

"Nah…" Pike said as he too enjoyed the beauty of the place. "We stopped comin' here right after Smoak was born."

Conversation rested between them. For a time, only the sounds of nature filled the air. There was the soft crush of grass beneath their shoes, the infrequent caw of some wild bird or the wind rustling the abundance of brush surrounding them.

Sabella; ever observant, began to frown the closer they got to the cabin. Her expressive chestnut stare narrowed and she raised a hand to her brow. When they were but a few feet from the porch, she stopped. "Isak?"

"Yeah, Babe?" Pike kept walking, pulling keys from his pocket as he took the porch steps three at a time.

Belle worried the edge of the wavy braid that lay across her shoulder. "Where are we?" She asked even as her expression registered faint recognition.

Pike grinned, scanning the key ring for the one he needed. "Don't worry, we aren't totally alone. Not much of the family visits out here anymore. The caretakers keep a calendar so nobody hordes in on anyone else's time."

"Is there a town nearby?"

"Sure there is- Kelowna."

Belle's mouth fell open.

"That was Okanagan Valley we flew over."

"Are you serious?" She thought the stretch of land had seemed familiar. They weren't that far from Vancouver. "You told me not to even think about going home." She reminded him.

"You're not home," he pointed out, smiling when he located the key he wanted. He unlocked the heavy pine door and waited for her to precede him inside.

Grand scale indeed. Belle thought as she stepped into the fragrant, warm cabin. Its earthy appeal was almost tangible. Decorated with overt Southwestern charm, gleaming pine floors ran throughout and were decorated by vibrantly designed throw rugs.

The same rich woodwork paneled the walls. The wide staircase around the corner from the foyer was carpeted by the same designs on the throw rugs. Oil murals decorated the walls and depicted images of the West when it was young and untamed. Other portraits showed fiercely beautiful Indian warriors on horseback.

Sabella appreciated the high ceilings, and the quality and detailed craftsmanship the home boasted. She strolled the entire lower level, taking note of wide stone hearths in each room (except the huge kitchen/ dining room/sitting room). Somehow, the place exuded airiness and coziness at once.

She was easing her hands into the side pockets of her denim skirt, when a thud caught her attention.

Pike had dumped their bags at the foot of the staircase. The bottomless dark of his stare commanded her silently as he leaned against one of the newel posts.

Belle smoothed her hands across the stylish straight skirt and walked slowly toward him. Her matching ankle length duster and black hand-crafted cowboy boots were more than appropriate for the brisk temperatures.

At least they *had* been. Now, she was positively roasting.

"Take this off," Pike motioned toward the duster after he'd taken a moment to rake her body with his affecting stare.

Belle obliged. She let the coat drop to pool about her boots.

"And this," he referred to her skirt. A devilish yet playful smirk curved his mouth as he took note of the way she pressed her lips together and blinked more than a little in response to his request. She wore sheer socks instead of hose and he couldn't have been more delighted.

"Very nice..." he whispered, tilting his head to observe her at his leisure. "Get rid of everything else. Not those," he added, referring then to the calf-high boots which hid her socks.

Belle knew her face would have surely been stained crimson had she been of a lighter complexion. The heat was absolutely sweltering by then. She hesitated once her fingers settled to the buttons on the long sleeved navy blouse she'd worn with the denim suit.

"Isak..."

"Do it." His deep, soft voice was more persuasive in the wake of desire filling the room.

Belle removed her panties first and Pike lost whatever restraint he had left. His gaze was fixed on the lacy undergarment as it slid down her legs, tangling about the boots before she stepped out of them. He pulled her to him before she could finish undoing her blouse.

AlTonya Washington

Sabella had only a quick second to bite her lip before his tongue was thrusting past. Sounds of lust and need surged between the lovers then. Pike had one hand beneath her shirt, cupping her ass while his free hand worked to undo her heavy braid.

Belle uttered consistent whimpers, her nails grazing the silky whiskers shadowing his face. She drove her tongue against his in an eager, erotic fashion. Standing on her toes, she linked her arms about his neck and increased the hungry element to her kiss.

Pike settled back next to the newel post and raised one of her legs just enough to give his free hand room to play.

"Mmm..." her moan wavered during the kiss. She could barely participate in their tongue-play then, unable to focus on anything other than him plundering the slick folds of her sex. Instinctively, she began to grind down on his fingers as they thrust and rotated three at a time inside her body.

The wavering moans she'd uttered throughout their kiss now merged in with gasps. She was on the verge of tears- the pleasure was that unreal, that missed, that incredible. Her hands flexed at his neck before they moved up to tighten in his hair. Belle trembled on the threshold of an orgasm but he stopped before she could step through.

"Isak!" her whisper carried on a tone of disbelief. "Don't," she begged, grabbing his hand to guide it back.

Pike turned the tables then. He took her legs from beneath her and carried her up the wide staircase in an effortless display of his power.

Belle murmured something indecipherable yet appreciative. She nuzzled his ear with her nose and then her tongue when he turned into the first bedroom he found. There, he dropped her on the bed and followed her down.

"Wait," she whispered, remembering her boots.

"Keep 'em on."

"What?" She almost laughed, until she took note of his fixed expression.

"I expect you to keep them on until I'm done with you. Understood?" He nodded minutely until she responded in kind.

Nodding was all she could have managed anyway. Her heart was lodged in the center of her throat and stifled the production of any words.

Pike graced her with a sly wink and a smile, brushing her jaw with his fist. He didn't waste time undoing the buttons of her shirt and simply ripped it open. Her bra was next.

"May I?" Belle asked before he could settle down over her.

Challenge lurking in the pitch depths of his stare, Pike shrugged. His laughter filled the spacious room when Belle returned the favor by whipping the gray and black checkered shirt from his back.

Ravenous for her, he caressed every part of her. He outlined her full, heavy breasts with the tip of his nose. He

smiled when she breathed in sharply while he buried his
face in the fragrant valley between them.

Belle shivered amidst the breathy massage his hair
provided when the onyx locks glided across her hands,
beneath her chin and over her chest.

Pike weighed and squeezed the pecan brown
mounds. Cupping them in his wide grasp, he pressed the
orbs close to his very handsome face and inhaled her
fragrance. She was thrusting her hips softly yet desperately
against his. She bit down on her lip again, stimulated by the
provocative friction of her bare sex nudging his behind the
jean's zipper.

Belle moved to free him from the denims and could
have sobbed when he pushed her hands aside. He took care
of the task, then lay down and pulled her over to straddle
him. The healthy wavy ribbons of her chestnut locks
curtained their faces when she leaned down to kiss him
sweetly.

Pike reached beneath the tails of her open shirt.
Cradling her bottom, he settled her beautifully, intimately.
Belle shuddered as though she'd been given a shot of
something she'd been craving wildly. Moments after she
began to ride him, he finished tearing the open shirt and bra
from her body. He wanted no obstacles hindering his
appraisal of her frame.

Sabella was too overtaken by sensation and want to
experience a shred of self doubt in the presence of the man
she made love to. Smoothing her hands up and down his

strong forearms, she felt awed by the chords of muscle rippling below the dark bronze of his flesh.

Pike bit down on his lip, praying he could hold out against her.

"Belle…" his tone sounded helpless, tortured, aroused. His deep set ebony stare absorbed the alluring tone of her skin. The missed feel of her as she bounced over him, the way her thick satiny thighs and bottom filled his greedy hands…he prayed very hard for the will to resist the demanding urges of his body.

His prayers went unanswered. Her exquisite face; partnered with her lush curves surrounding him and her tight drenched center gloving and releasing his erection, sent his need spewing.

"Fuck," he snapped wincing over the pleasure even while he cursed his loss of control. He squeezed her bottom tighter keeping her secure to fill her with his seed.

Belle's cries mingled with other breathless sounds of pleasure. She savored the warmth of the liquid filling her and pressed her hands to his where they covered her. Gradually, she slowed the movement of her hips. Intrigue filled the glowing pools of her gaze as she watched him come down off the high. She clenched her walls around his still throbbing shaft and smiled, taking delight in his reaction.

"Sorry…I'm sorry Bella…"

The intrigue in her eyes mixed with disbelief. He apologized as though what he'd done to her had been something less than incomparable. Sabella wondered how she'd survived the last seven years without him. Again, she leaned close to plant a sugary kiss to his mouth, pushed the hair back from his wide forehead and kissed him there too.

She eased off him gently and he grunted as if tortured in the nicest way. She tugged his earlobe and waited for him to open his eyes and look over at her.

"So can I take my boots off now?" She asked.

Quiet laughter filled the bedroom.

***

"Miss Carmen? He's asking for you."

Carmen set aside the two outfits she'd been debating over. "Thank you Jeri." She told the young maid who stood just inside the door of the elegant bedchamber.

Jeri offered a nod and smile. "Ma'am," she bowed her head before leaving.

Carmen puffed out her cheeks and observed the empty doorway with a sense of foreboding. She hadn't actually been serious about selecting the outfits. She simply needed something to occupy her time- her mind.

Besides, she and Jasper hadn't set foot outside since the previous afternoon. It had been that long since he'd spoken a word to her. It had been that long since she'd told him about the events of a long ago night. The night her entire world had been shockingly and violently turned inside out.

Of course Jasper couldn't be any more furious with her than she was with herself. Actually, she didn't *suppose* he could be any more furious with her. He was still the same sweet, subtle handsome guy she'd fallen in love with so long ago. Now though, that *guy* was protected by layers and layers of the man he'd become.

He was changed- no doubt. Then again, they all were. Time had been kind to them who the younger generation called The Elders. They'd certainly grown richer and yes more incredible to look at.

Carmen stopped to observe herself in the mirror above the carved oak dresser. The faint smile she managed faded. Time's *benefits* had stopped with outer beauty. Secrets had their own ways of taking tolls on one's body and soul. Carmen had a feeling both she and Jasper were just beginning to scratch each other's surfaces.

A shiver caused her to flinch and she reached for a wrap to cover her shoulders bared by the straps of her sundress. She'd told Jasper about the rape. Given his reaction, she regretted not telling him the rest of it. She hadn't told him of the pregnancy and knew that; more than anything would hit him hardest of all.

***

"When I said I was hungry, I was thinkin' salad."

"Mmm, salad…" Isak relaxed against the counter and continued to shake the glass decanter of his homemade dressing. "I was thinking food- *real* food."

Belle folded her arms across her chest. "Salad *is* real food."

"Doesn't put meat on your bones."

Smiling broadly, Belle patted her waistline hidden beneath the shirt she'd snatched from his back hours earlier. "I believe I've got quite enough, thanks."

"Not enough for me," Pike muttered, his voice dropping to an octave which proved he'd lost his taste for teasing.

"You don't have to live with it." Belle raised her chin a fraction when he sent her a stony look.

He slammed the decanter to the counter. "What is it with you and losing weight?"

"There's nothing about *me* and losing weight." She set her hands to her hips. "I didn't do it on purpose, Isak."

"Then what's up? Have you been sick?" His expression sharpened when he caught sight of the weariness she hadn't managed to keep from her expression.

"I *do* exercise on occasion, you know?" She sounded offended.

Pike sent a flourishing wave in her direction. "And your exercising is what brought on this new slim down?"

Sabella enjoyed almost a full minute of laughter. "Slim down?" She wiped a tear from her eye. "I'm a size eighteen!"

Pike rolled his eyes. "Eighteen?" He repeated the number as if it insulted him. "Size eighteen with legs up to your neck. You lose any more dress sizes and you'll be skinny as a rail."

Belle lost herself in another fit of giggles. "Could we just eat? Please?" She managed to ask, during the laugh attack.

"Gotta eat everything I put on your plate." He ordered like a parent to a child.

Belle cringed, but didn't balk over the idea. "What's for dinner?"

Pike placed the dressing to the table. "Vegetarian lasagna, chicken parm, sour dough rolls. Oh! And your salad."

"I can't…" Belle shook her head sending the loose ponytail into her face. "I *won't* eat half that Isak."

"That's fine." He calmly went about the task of bringing the food to the table. "I rather hear about your new weight loss regiment anyway. Is it healthy or is it part of some nasty side effect of somethin' you shouldn't be shoveling into your system?"

She blinked, her thoughts moving toward the pills for her panic attacks. The bottle had been out in plain sight at the hotel. He could've seen them…

Pike closed their distance. He walked over and braced his hands to either side of Belle where she stood before the L-shaped cutting board countertop.

"So? What'll it be?" His ebony eyes sparkled with challenge and a fair amount of suspicion. For more than a few moments, his gaze settled on her bra and panties visible past the ripped front of his shirt.

Meanwhile, Belle focused on the raised brand marring the otherwise flawless bronze of his bare chest. With effort, she looked toward the table he'd set for two.

"You said that was vegetarian lasagna?"

"Mmm hmm," he stepped back to let her pass. The challenge left his eyes when she took a chair. The suspicion however, remained and made way for concern.

NINE

Carmen didn't need to knock on the door to the office- it was already open. She stepped inside barely taking note of the intimidating, state-of-the-art room. She recalled asking Jasper what he needed a place like that for at a vacation getaway. He'd said he had a lot of pots on the stove and never knew when one might be ready to boil over.

She swallowed, watching him leaning against the front of his desk. His legs were crossed at the ankles and his arms were folded over his broad chest. The easy stance however, did nothing to hide the predatory aura which seemed to lurk about him. As Carmen studied him, she couldn't help but wonder about the manner in which he might tend to a boiling pot.

"Have a seat."

Carmen's hazel stare shifted toward one of the chairs flanking the desk. "I'll stand."

Anger flashed on Jasper's dark face. "Do you think I'd attack you like your ass of a brother?"

"No." She breathed the word while hurrying close to him.

Jasper took her upper arm and gave her a jerk. "Why the hell didn't you tell me?"

His voice seemed to crack on emotion and Carmen felt her heart break a little more. "I can't apologize for the way I saw fit to handle things."

He looked surprised. "Handle things? That's what you call it?"

"I didn't tell you for the same reason I never said anything to Westin or Damon." She smiled wryly thinking of her older brothers. "They would have killed Marcus quick without ever stopping to think of their own futures bright with success, happiness, love-"

"What about your own love and happiness?"

Carmen drew the wrap tighter about her shoulders. "Life's a funny thing," she said, her gaze bright in spite of the tears. "Even after what he did…I wound up having more love and happiness than I ever thought possible." She was thinking of Sabella then.

Jasper bowed his head. He'd read the tenderness in her eyes as love for another man.

Slowly, Carmen reached up to stroke the side of his face. "It's not what you think. Love and happiness come in many forms. Mine came in the form of an exquisite, exquisite baby girl."

Jasper's hands; still folded over Carmen's arms, tightened. His head bowed lower than before and what sounded like a gurgled scream rose from his throat. Love for her, anger for what she'd been through and heartache over how it had stalled their future all roiled together inside him.

"Shh…" Carmen stood on her toes and leaned close to kiss the top of his head. The silky crop of his hair was now a rich shade of silver. She felt him shaking and knew he'd fallen victim to the tears stirred by her confession.

"How Carm?" He spoke after what seemed like hours. "How could you have his child? Why would you have wanted to bring evil like that into the world?"

"Jasper," Carmen pressed her forehead to his jaw, "because she could have been yours."

He jerked away from her as if she burned to touch. "Mine? You don't know who she belongs to?"

Carmen hugged herself. "At first, I was afraid to know and then-then I just didn't want to. I love my girl with every part of me, but to know for *certain* that monster's blood was pumping through her veins…I haven't found the strength to risk it…yet."

Jasper stiffened and rose to his full height. "She could still have a monster's blood running through her veins and *not* be Marc's."

Carmen stiffened then too. She recognized the old argument. In that moment, she saw him as the worthless uncertain boy he'd been and she couldn't bear it. She moved close again, gripping his face and waiting for his eyes to meet hers. "You are not a monster."

"I'm not the boy you knew, Carm," his smile was pitiful yet his expression was haunted.

"The boy and the man are good," she argued.

"Many would disagree with you."

"Then many are wrong."

Some of the pity left Jasper's smile and he saw the girl who had made it her mission to save him so long ago.

"We should talk about Sabella."

"Sabella." Jasper repeated the name as if it had struck him suddenly and made the child real in his eyes.

"I prayed so long she was ours." Carmen leaned next to Jasper against the desk. "By the time she was born, I'd convinced myself that she was. I even gave her part of Miss Belle's name. She referred to Jasper's mother Belleina Stone. "No one made that connection though, except Bri. She's the only one I ever told, she knows everything.

She'd just named her own baby girl Sybilla after her mother." Carmen smiled, thinking of her sister-in-law.

"Miss Sybil." Jasper recalled Bri's mother, a woman who'd been so kind to him in the horrible days of his youth.

"Anyway…" Carmen scooted into a sitting position on top of the neat desk. "Everyone just thought she was yours."

"Hmph and I bet they hated me for leaving you."

Carmen shook her head. "I made sure they understood it was my decision and that I just wasn't ready to be a wife. There was too much I wanted to do- too much I wanted to show my daughter." She shrugged and tugged on the tassels of the silk coral wrap. "They believed it, with Bri's help."

Jasper left his place at the desk and moved to the window that overlooked the eastern portion of his property. "What's she like?"

"Beautiful." Carmen said without hesitation and then shrugged again. "But that's obvious to see when you look at her. She's got that beauty that can only come from the soul. It's true." She said when Jasper looked her way. "There's something cool…elegant-above anything petty. She's so much like Mama."

Jasper smiled as the image of yet another kind-hearted and magnificent woman came to mind. Marcella Ramsey had diligently seen to his welfare after the passing of his mother.

"There's just something about her…" Carmen went on. "The other kids practically revere her and she's not

even the oldest of them. Guess I'm just letting pride get in
the way but I don't think I'm overstating it *too* much."

"Not too much." Jasper's words were as soft as the
look in his eyes. No one could doubt the woman's love for
her child in spite of how she'd come into the world.

"Nothing can make me believe Marcus had any part
in creating her," Carmen's features tightened defiantly.

"Then why not find out for sure?"

"Because I know how cruel fate can be. The *not*
knowing kept me sane."

"Does *he* know?"

Carmen shook her head. "I don't know. He hasn't
spoken of it and I haven't been completely alone with him
since that night. He's conveniently absent from any family
gatherings I attend. I forbid anyone to let him near Belle.
No one ever questioned it." She offered up a smug smile
then. "They didn't much want their own kids around him
either. Hell that even went for his own wife." She thought
of Josephine then.

"So why are you telling me now?" Jasper rested on
the reinforced window pane.

"That's why I've been keeping Marcus alive- I
didn't want him dead before I told you the truth- all of it.
All this time, I've let you believe I wanted him to suffer
because of all the trouble he's caused for the family...
Besides, torturing the evil bastard has been very therapeutic
and I wanted you to experience it."

Jasper's smile seemed to hint at his anticipation. "Why'd you wait to tell me? We've been together three years."

"Because I was selfish," Carmen studied the life lines in her palms. "You can hate me for that if you want-you'd be right to hate me for it. These three years have been like a dream and I've been so happy." She clasped her hands together and kept them in her lap. "I wanted to enjoy it for as long as I could. Then there was Belle," she looked over at Jasper.

"She was in such a bad way...broken up with her husband-it almost ruined her." Briefly, Carmen closed her eyes on the memory. "No one saw it coming. She and Isak were so happy. She never told me what really happened there. About three or four years ago Belle turned it all around just like that. It looked like she was finally getting past the break up."

Carmen smoothed both hands over her face and kept them there for a time. "I couldn't do it Jasper I just couldn't. And then..." she eased off the desk. "The guilt started in- worse than it'd ever been. I-" She turned toward him. "I needed you to know if only for support when I tell her.

I never expect your forgiveness but I need you...I- I need you to be with me when I tell her because I don't have the courage to do it on my own and-" she hugged herself as though a sudden thought had chilled her. "Belle's sure to hate me when she finds out and she'd have every right to. Just like you."

A Lover's Shame

Jasper offered no reply and only stood stoically next to the window. Carmen gave a slight nod, accepting that there was nothing more to be said. She was halfway to the door when he spoke.

"She won't hate you."

He left his post by the window as Carmen turned to face him.

"If she's mine, then she won't hate you because *I* don't hate you."

Emotions swelled again and Carmen ran to Jasper. She clutched him in a desperate embrace.

***

Morning found Sabella before the L-shaped counter again. She'd added cream to a mug of hot coffee and stood watching the black brew turn an inviting shade of beige. She was adding sugar and stirring the liquid when a wall of muscle pressed in close and heated behind her. Her lashes fell momentarily over her eyes and her fingers tightened on the spoon handle. She bit her upper lip to keep a moan suppressed.

Pike was grazing the nape of her neck- bare thanks to her messy ponytail. "Forgive me." He murmured the words into her skin while easing both hands around her front to slip inside her robe.

Belle abandoned her coffee. She turned, standing on her toes and curling her fingers into the satiny onyx whiskers that shadowed his face.

"You have nothing to apologize for." Her voice was soft but the order was firm. "This is all about me, all of it. I'm to blame-"

"Stop," He shook his head.

Belle could detect the stirrings of something enraged filling his gaze as if he were sickened to hear her taking responsibility for all that had happened. She rested her hands on his forearms, tracing the chords lining them while she considered her words.

"I'm on medication- pills."

"I think you know I'm already aware of that." He patted her hip once. "What are they for?"

"Um…panic attacks. The job um…so much stress- it got to me." She lied. To tell him the attacks started when she left him would lead to questions she couldn't (wouldn't) answer.

"I had a lot to prove then- that I was there because I deserved to be and not because of my last name."

Pike's fingers strummed a silent tune along her back, covered by the sheer robe. He let her think he bought the story of what had started the attacks. The fact that she'd told him about the pills at all was progress within itself. His bottomless gaze was unreadable as it searched her face.

It took a bit of doing for Belle to summon courage to meet his eyes. When she was finally able to do so, she blinked struck by the intensity of his stare.

"Are these pills causing you to lose weight?"

A Lover's Shame

Belle didn't hold back her quick nod. "It's a side effect- a good one if you ask me." She looked away when his gaze narrowed.

"I think it stinks."

"Well I don't expect you to understand it." She watched him bow his head and couldn't look away from the muscle he worked along his jaw. When he looked her way again, his expression had grown softer.

"Kiss me," he commanded.

Belle moved to her toes again and eagerly obliged. The kiss began sweetly and turned lusty in the breadth of two seconds. She curled her fingers into the low rise waistband of his sleep pants and forgot everything except who held her and what she wanted from him.

His touch ventured beneath the scant robe to play with her sex and she tensed. Pike pulled back, suspicion registering on his face.

"Have I been hurting you?" He asked.

Her cheeks burned while she fought to smother a moan. Images of the varied and erotic things they'd been doing somersaulted to the front of her mind.

"Bella?"

"A little tender, that's all."

Pike smoothed her cheek against his before perfectly sculpted lips glided the line of her neck and collarbone. "I'll have to be more careful with you then."

"No please," she gasped before realizing what she was saying. She'd welcomed everything he'd done to her and couldn't accept him stopping or changing his methods.

Pike's soft chuckling showed no signs of settling when he pulled her into a tight hug.

***

"What the hell?" Quest sat frowning murderously over the folder he held. He was barely half way through the massive weapons division report, yet things looked all on the level.

Quest had hoped to be done with the report by the time Mick came home to him. He grimaced, massaging his eyes while trying to cast the thought of his wife from his head. No such luck there, but he did manage to set her just a bit farther from the front of his conscience. Any closer and he could forget about finishing the report or anything else work related.

Unfortunately, the report had him stumped. Strange notes in the margins were written in Drake's familiar yet illegible scrawl.

As sitting there wasting time wasn't doing a damn bit of good for his mood, Quest reached for the phone and dialed the Switzerland office. He was connected to the office of the COO within a matter of seconds.

"...and we still haven't gotten the numbers for that particular department. We're still haggling over a few details."

"Mmm hmm..." Quest made his own notes while Drake went on about the research issues. "Hold on- *research issues?*"

"Yeah…the scientists are screaming bloody murder over their rights to the research."

Quest shook his head. "So much for this goin' smooth," he murmured.

"Well it's only a matter of time and money before we get it all squared away."

"So is everything else on track?" Quest jotted a few more notes. "Drake?" He called when the man didn't rebut with a quick 'yes'.

"Yes and no, Q."

"Shit," Quest tossed the pen across his desk. "What?"

"Well I'd hoped to have more details before coming to you with this."

"Just spill it Drake."

"It's about the sale of our weapons cache in the South Pacific. Our people there didn't follow your instructions to the letter about the terms of the sale."

"Jesus Drake, English please."

"Right, right…" Drake cleared his throat. "It seems the weapons there were sold to a private entity instead of our military contacts."

"Hell," Quest groaned, leaning back in his chair and refusing to acknowledge the old fraternity brand aching his arm. "Drake please tell me we haven't just provided weapons for some warlord's crusade?"

Drake tried to laugh, but couldn't. "They haven't gone towards that, I promise you."

"Well do we at least know who we sold them to?"

AlTonya Washington

Again, Drake tried to laugh. "Trust me Q, after I tell you, you may just wish they'd gone to the warlord."

Quest massaged his aching arm then.

TEN

Because it was there and because they were practically in total seclusion and because Pike had bullied her into a terribly fattening breakfast hours earlier, Belle decided to enjoy a mid-morning swim in the nude. She'd been on the go so much with the play her treasured pastime/workout had been ignored for far too long.

Pike had business to handle on the phone. Shortly after breakfast, Belle headed for the figure 8 shaped in ground set off in its own area and shielded by a wealth of

AlTonya Washington

shade providing trees. She was slipping a cover-up over her otherwise nude body when a long whistle caught her ears.

"Please tell me I didn't miss whatever it is you're about to do."

Belle laughed over Pike's question. "I've already done it, sorry."

The expectancy in his dark eyes mingled with devilment and curiosity. "What was it?"

"Just a swim."

"In that?" He nodded toward the sheer cover up.

"In what's beneath it."

"And what is that?"

"Nothing."

Pike clutched his heart in a playfully hurt manner and then went about spreading a blanket down in front of the trees sheltering the pool area.

"So what's that?" She cast a speculative eye towards the basket he'd brought along.

"Our lunch."

Belle couldn't have been more stunned. "But we just ate breakfast."

"And now it's time for lunch."

"Isak...don't you want me to be healthy?"

"That's why I'm feeding you," his tone was matter-of-fact while he set about hammering down the wooden stakes to secure the blanket.

"I don't buy that these pills for panic attacks are affecting your weight like that unless you haven't been eating and I can tell by the way you pick at your food that you haven't been."

"Lots of people have crazy eating habits when they're crazy busy, Isak."

"Mmm they do, but that's not what this is about, is it?"

Belle shook her head when he faced her with challenge in his eyes. "I can't believe you," her hands hit her thighs in a single slap. "Most men would be happy as a clam to have a woman who's…"

"What? Skinny as a stick and slippin' through his fingers when he's tryin' to make love to her? No thanks."

She watched him finish with the blanket and begin setting out the lunch he'd brought. "Miss Immi's gorgeous and tall and *slender* and-"

"Exactly what my father likes and you're exactly what *I* like." He paused over the basket to let his onyx stare glide over her in repeated appreciative strokes.

Belle rolled her eyes and plopped down to the hunter green and burgundy checkered blanket. Pike made pretence at unpacking the basket but he was more interested in watching her. She leaned back on her hands and tilted her head as the wind caught her hair and lifted the wavy strands about her face. When she lay on her back, he pounced.

Her arms came around his lean waist seconds after he settled over her. He'd exasperated her to no end, but there was no way she could ever be truly angry with him. She arched her neck when his mouth glided across her jaw.

Perfect teeth latched onto the silver tab of the zipper securing her cover up.

"You know what a good cook I am," he tugged down her zipper while voicing the reminder.

"That's the problem- mmm..." She arched a bit more when his nose dipped between her breasts. "If you want me to be healthy, I know other ways."

"So do I."

Belle felt her heart stop in her throat at the wicked glance he threw her way. He continued tugging down the tab until it'd reached her navel. Resting between her thighs then, Pike began an intimate assault on her nipples. His fingers manipulated one while his lips and tongue handled the other.

The dual caress sent a jolt of sensation through Belle. She tried to keep her eyes open, but she was virtually hypnotized by the sway of the tree limbs overhead. Her lashes fluttering were as much affected by them as they were by Pike's touch.

Hushed whimpers slipped past her parted lips. He was suckling ravenously on her nipple then. His fingers had managed to work its twin into a rigid bud that puckered and silently begged for more care. As though it'd called to him, Pike switched his attention to it.

Sabella ground her hips against him. She was caught between wanting to funnel her fingers through his hair or hers. The hushed whimpering gained volume as the breeze chilled the nipple he'd left wet and abandoned. Pike captured her wrists and kept her hands at her sides. The only movement he allowed was the suggestive writhing of her hips. Intermittently, he nibbled and sucked, circling his nose about the generous curve of one breast and then the other.

Trembling fiercely by then, Belle knew she was on the verge of climax. Pike however, refused to accommodate her need. He deserted her chest, dropped kisses to her stomach and briefly tongued her navel. His dimples emerged beneath the whiskers covering his jaw when her laughter mingled with a gasp. He moved lower, to the bare triangular patch of skin above her sex.

His hands flexed on her derriere while he inhaled her scent. He was already powerfully aroused and her smell threatened to send him right over the edge. He outlined her vulva with the tip of his nose and had to tighten his hold on her thighs when she jerked violently beneath him. For a while, he worked his nose along that part of her anatomy.

Belle, trapped in the power of his hold and foreplay, cried out into the fragrant remote environment and begged him not to stop. Her entire body shuddered wildly when his tongue darted out to saturate the petals of her femininity before his lips applied more proper care. She wasn't shy about crying out as the sensations built one on top of the other.

Pike released her wrists and desperately Belle sank her fingers into the glossy darkness of his hair. "Mmm…" she drove herself softly yet wantonly against his mouth. His tongue was deep inside her and thrusting with a scandalous intensity.

When he rose up suddenly, Belle blinked and was seconds from screaming her frustration. He'd only moved to tug the lightweight sweatshirt over his head. Her eyes widened in appreciation of the carved beauty and breadth of his torso.

The sun was high that afternoon. The beaming rays turned his skin a shade of molten gold. The sinews of his arms, abs and chest flexed; in a manner that was as much an aphrodisiac as the steady glint of his eyes.

Pike had tossed his shirt over the food basket and relaxed over what he preferred to dine on.

"Isak…" Belle lost her fingers in his hair again. "Isak…Isak…" she chanted as he ravaged the sensitized softness of her labia. "Mmm…" her moan was shaky as he spread her sex with strong fingers and hungrily feasted.

A tidal wave of sensation swept her again but she didn't want it to end. She tensed as the sensual wave crested on desire and relaxed when it settled into pleasure.

Pike could feel her clenching and releasing his tongue and he increased the depth of the intimate kiss. Belle kept her fingers clenched tight in his hair in case he had any thoughts of stopping. Restlessly, she moved her thighs back and forth across his whiskered cheeks and luxuriated in the rough, sensational feel of it.

Climax hit her hard, unrelenting in its vibrancy. Her hands trembled too badly to maintain their hold on Pike and fell away. He withdrew from the very personal kiss and began to press shallow ones to the hollow of her inner thigh. He lavished their fleshy expanse with the same attention. The black deep gaze was riveted on her. Pike felt his ego hum at the sight of her in the throes of the orgasm he was responsible for. He settled over her again as her shudders started to wane.

Dropping kisses, Pike made his way up her body until his lips were on hers. Belle's response to the act was eager and immediate. As though she were addicted, she thrust her tongue back against his-drinking him in. Need swelled inside her-renewed by the taste of her body on his mouth.

Eventually, it was Pike who brought an end to the kiss. Briefly, he nuzzled her nose with his and then moved to gnaw at her neck.

"Now that I've eaten," he murmured near the pulse point at her throat, "it's your turn." He smiled when she laughed.

Sabella's amusement died though when she realized that he didn't intend for her to dine on him but the lunch he'd packed. She tossed a pebble at his back when he moved to prepare her plate.

***

Outside Mt. Kisko, New York~

"God, you get more incredible to look at every time I see you." Pitch Tesano's rough voice could best be described as a growl when he tugged his brother's wife close.

Imani Kamande Tesano's long black stare twinkled in a playfully wicked fashion as she studied her brother-in-law. "You should stop laying it on so thick. There aren't many ways for a woman to look *incredible* in a wheelchair."

"To hell with that," Pitch muttered and pulled back a bit but continued to kneel before her. "Whoever was stupid enough to think that never saw you," He tilted back his chin and frowned a bit. "How are you really?"

"I've never been better."

"My little brother treatin' you alright?"

"*Very* alright."

"Damn," Pitch feigned disgust. "Oh well," he sighed and pulled Imani into another hug and kiss.

"One hug and one kiss is enough." Roman called on his way down the front staircase.

Pitch muttered something while waving off his brother. He held Imani's chin between his thumb and forefinger. "Don't you go missing before I leave."

"I promise," Imani rubbed the back of her hand along the side of the man's beautifully crafted dark copper-toned face. When she moved close for a third kiss, her husband cleared his throat.

"Hey what'd I say, man?" Roman cast a playfully outraged glare at Pitch.

"It's *her* doin'." Pitch argued while standing. "Hell, what's a man supposed to do when a gorgeous woman kisses him?" He grumbled while walking away to the sound of Roman's and Imani's laughter.

A Lover's Shame

It was Roman's turn to kneel before his wife. "We've got some business. Just some stuff to clear up. I shouldn't be long…"

Imani shook her head. Explanations were completely unnecessary especially since Roman wasn't even leaving the house. However, as her husband was obsessively attentive, Imani knew there was nothing she could say that would change his ways after all the years that had passed between them.

Roman moved up to kiss her. It was only intended to be a peck, but she curled her hands into the collar of his sweater and kept him near as the kiss heated. Seconds later, she was pulling away.

Roman's unsettling dark eyes reflected…something but he wasn't about to question such a kiss. "I won't be long," he brushed his thumb across her flawless blackberry cheek and left to find his brother.

"So how's she really doin'?" Pitch asked once Roman reached the study door where he was waiting.

"She's good. Good." Roman confirmed, yet the very long straight brows above his gaze drew close into the slightest of frowns. "At least that's what she tells me."

Pitch nodded, easily observing the concern hardening his brother's profile. He gave Roman's back a hard clap. "Let's talk," he said.

Silence held between the brothers as they made their way into Roman's study/rec room/den/kitchenette. There were all the comforts of home and practically every necessity for a man with an unending stream of interests. Soon, the brothers were settled in with sandwiches and their favorite brews.

"Unless Gabriel's one hell of an actor, he don't know a damn thing." Pitch spoke around a mouthful of salami on rye then followed it and his words with a swig of Guinness.

"Remember this is Grekka we're talkin' about." Roman slanted Pitch a wink.

Pitch laughed over Roman's use of the nickname that stuck between all the brothers. For Roman and Vale; the youngest, it was their best pronunciation of the name. Gabriel seemed to adore it, so everyone was happy.

"Don't misunderstand me, Rome. Gabriel knows plenty but not about why Marc's out at Brogue's place."

"I still don't like it."

"Neither do it." Pitch threw back another healthy swig of the dark beer. "That's one hell of a dysfunctional relationship but Gabe and his little boy are close."

Roman focused on the remnants of his Sam Adams. "So do you really believe the kid hasn't talked about it?"

Pitch took another monstrous bite of his sandwich. "No love lost between the two of 'em but hell Rome...I pried every which way from Sunday without comin' right out and asking what I wanted to know. Gabe answered every question- never once told me to get the fuck out of his office. Now what does that tell you?"

Roman shrugged. "That he's starting to love you a little?" He finished his drink while his brother chuckled.

"Seriously Rome?" Pitch encouraged once the laughter softened.

"That he was too preoccupied to realize you were fishin'."

"Definitely," Pitch set aside the empty plate and balanced the beer can on a denim-clad knee.

"Well hell, there's always somethin' goin' on with the family- could be a bunch of petty shit that has him absent minded."

"Could be."

"So how long are you gonna dick around before tellin' me whatever it is you suspect?"

"That depends on how deep into the crap you're ready to go."

"How deep?" Roman appeared more dangerous when his gaze narrowed. "I've been deep in the crap before."

"Mmm hmm and before you were *encouraged* to let it go."

Roman bowed his head for almost a full minute. When he looked up again, the dangerous tint to his stare was mixed with a more heated element. "I don't need you reminding me of that."

"Calm down." Pitch left his chair to deposit the empty paper plate and beer can into the wastebasket. He clapped Roman's shoulder on his way past. "I'm not out to bring up bad memories here, but you had to pay dearly for that diggin' around. The stakes could be just as high this time if not more so. You may not like where this goes."

"I need to know what this is. You let *me* worry about the rest."

Pitch folded his arms across his wide chest and studied Roman until he was convinced. "How surprised would you be if I told you I picked up where you left off?"

"I'd say what the hell for?" Roman frowned watching from his chair as Pitch headed back toward the kitchenette. "All I had was a bunch of speculation."

"And yet somebody tried to kill you over it."

Roman left his chair then. He unconsciously clenched his fists and closed his eyes to pray that the dark emotions rising within him wouldn't take hold.

"Rome?"

"What else?"

Pitch tapped out a slow tune against the mini-bar and debated before proceeding cautiously. "What if I told you your speculation might be mixed with a nice amount of fact?"

Roman Tesano wasn't a man to shock easily yet the expression he wore then was hard to categorize as anything else.

Pitch rummaged around in the mini-fridge. "Another beer?" He asked his brother.

***

A Lover's Shame

Vancouver, Canada~

"Oh my God…" Belle felt like a kid taking in her first circus. It was an awesome sight to view her apartment building from the air and even more awesome to be set down right in the center of the roof.

"Why didn't you tell me you were gonna do this?"

Pike only smiled when Belle followed her question with a punch to his thigh.

Sabella kept her eyes wide as he guided the chopper closer to its destination. Like before, she waited for him to come round and open her side. When she would have rushed out, he blocked her way.

"Half the fun in impressing someone, is surprising them." He told her, freeing a trapped lock of hair from the upturned collar of her quarter-length trench.

"You don't need to impress me, Isak. You know that."

"I disagree."

"But Isak, I don't deserve-" her words were silenced when his mouth fell on hers in a punishing kiss. She melted, fingers curling into the fleece of the jacket he sported. She was encircling her arms about his neck, when he suddenly jerked her back.

"Don't ever say that to me again. Don't ever talk to me about what you don't deserve, understood?"

"I-"

"Understood?" He waited for her nod, dropped a kiss to her forehead and was turning to greet the building manager as if he'd sensed the man's approach.

"Mr. Hermes thanks for approving the landing."

Georgian Hermes' toothy grin was broad as he shook hands with Isak. "No request is too unreasonable especially for the owner of the building."

Pike's smile was in response to the gasp only he heard Sabella utter.

"Ms. Ramsey. Welcome home."

She managed a quick smile. "Thanks Georgian. It's good to see you."

"Let's get in out of this wind, shall we?" Georgian turned to escort them from the rooftop.

Pike offered Belle his arm and she accepted after only the slightest hesitation.

"Still impressing me?" She asked once they were alone in the elevator headed to her floor.

Hands hidden in the pockets of sandstone carpenter's jeans, Pike only shrugged. His expression wasn't quite as cool as his stance unfortunately. Through the heavy fringe of his lashes, he watched her absorb the discovery she'd just made.

"When did you buy the building?"

"The day you moved in." He reached inside a pocket and withdrew his mobile before she could say another word.

A Lover's Shame

Belle lost herself in her thoughts. She could've remained there were it not for the call Pike made. Her lips parted in surprise and soon she appeared as though she were looking at a man she didn't recognize. Whoever was on the other end of the line had to be shaking in a fair amount of anger...or fear.

"...I don't pay you to be late, I pay you to wait. If I get a repeat performance of that shit back in Portland, it'd be best for you not to show up at all and to pray I never find you. Am I fuckin' understood?" he didn't wait for a response and shut down the phone.

Belle reminded herself to blink and look away. The soft depth of his voice; as he delivered the threat, sounded more menacing than if he'd bellowed the words.

The elevator doors opened then. When Pike waved a hand, Belle moved without hesitation.

AlTonya Washington

ELEVEN

"Get packed."

Belle's happiness over being returned to her stomping ground was short-lived.

"Where are we going?" She raised her chin silently informing him that she was sticking to her guns when he threw her a look.

"It's not unreasonable that I'd want to know, Isak."

"Where're the rest of your cases?" He nodded when she refused to answer him. "We're goin' somewhere I should've taken you a long time ago." He spread his hands

A Lover's Shame

as if to say that explanation would have to suffice. He took a chance on checking the coat closet for suitcases and gave a long whistle when his haunch proved correct.

Sabella blinked, forgetting her questions regarding their destination when he pulled the set of Louis Vuitton cases from the closet.

"Those aren't mine," she hurried over but stopped in her tracks when he straightened before the cases.

"Not yours? Then whose?"

Sweltering inside her coat, Belle tugged it off and tossed it the sofa. "The bags are mine but… not the ones I want to take." She coughed on the last few words.

"Really?" Long sleek brows raised a notch above the bottomless depths of his eyes. "And why's that?"

"Um…"

"Yes?"

"I was gonna get together with Sabra." She dropped to the sofa and fiddled with the oversized buttons on the plum coat. "We were gonna hook up after Fernando's wedding- after the season ended with the play, um…"

Pike eased both hands into his pockets and waited.

"So anyway, Sabra insisted on getting me a new wardrobe. She had everything picked out- pants to panties…" she rolled her eyes toward the bags. "She had it all sent up months ago. I haven't had the nerve to check out any of it, but if you know Sabra's taste in clothes… it doesn't take much to guess that stuff isn't suitable for anyplace except Vegas."

"Sabra…" Pike breathed, realizing he'd been holding his breath while thoughts of his ex-wife running off with another man filled his mind.

Belle didn't seem to notice his reaction. "It won't take me long to pack. Might help to know exactly where you're taking me, though." She grumbled on her way past the coffee table.

Pike snapped to. "Forget about it- these'll do fine."

"Uh-no," Belle laughed shortly and cast another glare towards the cases. "I love my cousin a lot, but we've never had the same taste in clothes." She gestured towards the chic gold skirt suit she wore with equally chic platform pumps. "God willing, we never will. I already came up with an excuse to give for forgetting them when I finally go see her."

"There'll be hell to pay if you forget them." Pike reminded her as his lips twitched on a smile.

Belle shrugged. "So be it. My body wasn't made for stuff like that."

"This shit again," Pike bristled. He left the bags and crossed the distance to her. "Would you wear them for me?"

"Definitely no," she shoved his chest and refused to dwell on how incredible he felt beneath her hands.

"It'd prepare you for Vegas." He reasoned.

"I'd rather wear them in Vegas, than for you." Her heart flipped at the disappointment she saw flash in his eyes. "Isak please, it wouldn't be a good idea. Trust me."

A Lover's Shame

"Do you think I'd see too much?" He smiled. "Have you forgotten everything we've been doing the last three days?"

"No." She swallowed. The word hinged on a moan and forced her to look away. "I can tell you without a shadow of a doubt that nothing in those bags is appropriate for wherever it is you're taking me."

"Maybe I'm taking you someplace where it'd just be the two of us."

"Haven't we had enough time alone?"

"Not nearly enough."

"Isak…" She folded her arms beneath her breasts and let her head fall back. "This won't turn out the way you think."

He went back toward the cases. "Let's go."

"What are you trying to do?" She groaned and then retreated when he kicked one of the cases across the floor and bolted towards her.

"I'm tryin' like hell to get my wife back."

"Your wife's gone."

"No. She's just lost beneath a whole lot of shit she won't share with me."

"You may be sorry you asked if she ever did."

Pike bowed his head and Belle held her breath when she glimpsed the rigid set to his profile. Thankfully, the tension was cut by the door bell ringing. Belle went to answer as though her salvation waited on the other side.

A petite Caucasian woman waited in the hall. Her dark blonde hair stood on end as if she'd been frantically running her fingers through it. The weariness in her pale blue eyes merged into one of hope when she looked up at Belle.

"Hey Rachel-" Before Belle could finish the greeting, the woman had pulled her into a crushing hug.

"Oh Belle, thank God, thank God," Rachel Hopman chanted, her eyes were shut tightly as she smiled.

"Rachel?" Belle disentangled herself from the woman's grip and stood back to study her. "What's wrong? Is it Kelly?" She asked, referring to Rachel's daughter.

Again, Rachel closed her eyes but a measure of relief filled the gesture. "She's fine. She's fine, I'm sorry."

Belle squeezed Rachel's hands as she too experienced relief. "What's wrong?"

"I'm sorry for acting so zoned out. I've been calling the front office every day for the last week asking if they knew when you'd be back."

"Well come on in." Belle moved from the door, still not caring for the uneasy expression her neighbor wore.

"Kelly was showing off the prom dress you made her. Dancing around in her room with her friends and snagged the damn thing from the hem to just under the armpit." Rachel ran her hands across the seat of her sweatpants and then dragged them through her hair. "She's driving me crazy, Belle. I swear I'm about to-"

Belle didn't need to ask what or *who* had rendered the woman speechless.

"Rachel? Blink?" Belle snapped her fingers before the woman's face. "Breathe." She gently commanded.

"Right," Rachel breathed and even managed a slow nod.

"Rachel Hopman, Isak Tesano." Belle turned and made the introductions.

Pike stepped close to take Rachel's hand. "Miss Hopman. Can I get you anything? Water, maybe?"

"Um…" Rachel was nodding but had yet to blink. "Water would be…fantastic."

Belle focused on the carpet in an attempt to hide her smile.

Pike squeezed Rachel's hand between both of his. "Be back in a sec." He slanted Belle a wink before taking his leave.

When he'd disappeared into the kitchen, Rachel whirled around to face Belle. Her mouth was an exact replica of the letter O.

Sabella knew her earlier introduction would require much more detail. Defensively, she raised her hands. "It's not what you're thinking."

"Liar. Who *is* he?"

"It's a long story."

Rachel cast a suggestive glance toward the kitchen door. "I'll bet." She said.

"Could you please get your mind out of your panties and back on your child?"

The advisement returned Rachel to the throes of anxiety. "I swear that girl…she's hysterical. Won't let me take the dress anywhere else to have it mended and as close as I am to the brink of insanity, I think it's best to carry it back to the source." She sent a flourishing wave toward Belle and sighed. "I'm so sorry about this. I know you've got better things to do than work on some kid's prom dress."

"Hey? Stop, alright?" Belle moved close to squeeze Rachel's arm. "That kid's *your* kid and she's a sweetie. This is in spite of the fact that she doesn't know how to dance in high fashion. Of course I'll mend it." She winked, smiling when her tease brought contentment to Rachel's expression.

"I'll pay whatever you ask-"

"Would you *please* stop?" Belle's voice crept on the tiniest bit of frustration then. "I didn't ask you to pay me for making it- why should you pay for repairs?"

The single mom practically melted then, awash in relief and gratitude. "Belle..." Was all she could say while moving in for another hug.

Pike had long since finished getting water from the kitchen. He hung back, not wanting to interrupt Sabella while she spoke with her friend. Earlier, she'd asked what he'd been trying to do and he'd said he'd been trying to get his wife back. That was only half of it.

To say he'd missed her was an understatement. He'd yearned for her, dreamed of her, cried over her- though he'd forbid himself to cry again after that first time...

He'd raged over the loss of her. Oh yes, more than anything he'd raged. More than all of that however, he'd loved her. During the past several days with her, that emotion had only intensified.

She was the most amazing and lovely thing that had ever come into his life. Nothing would ever make him believe a monster like Marcus Ramsey could claim her as his child.

Rachel caught sight of him lurking and Pike headed over with the water. She accepted it like a woman dying of thirst.

Belle tilted her head, urging him to the side for a bit of privacy. "Rachel's daughter needs a repair on the prom dress I made for her. It shouldn't be long but I've got to take care of it before we go."

He shrugged. "Take as much time as you need."

Belle pressed her lips together and fixed him with a skeptical look. "What about the people you've got waiting on us?"

"That's what they get paid for." He tugged the sleeve of her jacket. "Don't worry we'll have plenty of time to get back to our conversation."

"Right..." She recalled the topic they'd been in the middle of when the bell rang. She tried to read the look in his eyes and figured it was useless. "Rachel? Let's get goin'. I just need to grab my stuff." She headed to the coat closet for the mini sewing machine and her bag of accessories.

"It was nice meeting you." Pike told Rachel when she handed him her glass.

"Very *very* nice meeting you, Mr. Tesano."

"Please. All my friends call me Pike."

Rachel let her eyes wander and enjoy. "I'm sure they do." The words were almost a purr.

"This way…" Belle turned Rachel toward the door and hustled her out into the hall. She glanced across her shoulder in time to see Pike covering his mouth as he grinned.

***

Los Angeles, California~

Michaela Ramsey was completely impressed. She whistled while strolling the third floor which housed the gallery where Nile's kids showcased the work they created at the studio to foster their talents.

"Are you sure a group of teenagers did this?"

Nile laughed while checking messages from her office computer. "For the fifth time, I'm sure."

"You know…you should have a thing here." Mick suggested, easing both hands into the back pockets of her jeans as she studied the spacious gallery/loft/office.

A playful frown settled to Nile's dark oval face. "A *thing*?"

"A party. Something to show off the kids. Growing up the way some of them do, I can imagine how much it'd mean to have folks rave over the good they do instead of the bad."

A knowing smile crossed Nile's face as she listened. She could very well understand where Mick was coming from given her upbringing.

"Sorry." Mick closed her eyes and clasped all ten fingers through her curly locks. "Didn't mean to jump on my soapbox there."

"Oh please," Nile pushed back from her desk. "It's a great idea."

"Just that it's so incredible to see stuff like this… this gallery and the stuff Ramsey does to look out for kids. Quest and Quay were working on the teen center in Malibu when we met." She hugged herself and whirled around to fix Nile with an incredulous look. "Can you believe that? In Malibu?" She shook her head and went back to strolling the loft. "I never believed people existed who cared *that* much."

Nile came to sit on the edge of her desk. "Lots of people care and they all show it in different ways."

"Yeah…I guess I can include our family in that too, huh?" Again Mick shook her head and appeared to shiver. "That still sounds so weird… family."

"It's still new. Besides, they're a pretty outrageous group, it's going to take you some getting used to."

Michaela laughed then, thinking of the family she never knew she had. "They're gonna spoil Quinn more than she already is."

"Mmm…well I think kids should be spoiled."

Mick gave a firm nod. "Agreed. Thank you for bringing me here."

"And you know how little *I* had to do with it."

"Hmph." Mick recalled the woman who'd brought her and her sister into one another's lives.

Nile read the emotion on Mick's face and wanted nothing to mar the special time they'd enjoyed. "So about this idea of yours…"

Mick's expression returned to the bright side. "I mean, this is all so awesome it could be an incredible event. We could even bring Melina in on it."

"Mel…" Nile thought it over.

Mick came to sit on the other end of the desk. "Well you know she runs that huge gallery at home?"

Nile appeared doubtful. "She wouldn't be interested in hosting an art party for a bunch of kids though."

"Are you kidding? Charm Galleries is always looking for new and interesting ways to contribute." Mick snapped her fingers once. "Have you already forgotten that show she put on for you last year?"

"Last year," Nile breathed the words, her onyx stare taking on a faraway glint as she remembered the event. More had occurred than a simple showing to raise money for her studio.

"Sorry," Mick bit her lip, knowing Nile was remembering the dramatic and near fatal moments of the evening.

"It's alright," she reached for Mick's hand and squeezed. "Do you think it's really all over now?"

Mick focused on her fingers entwined with Nile's. "I want to believe it is."

"But do you really?"

"Guess I'm afraid to say so with absolute certainty."

A Lover's Shame

"Because; with this group, there always *is* something?"

Mick lifted her amber stare to Nile's face and shrugged. "Guess that's just the nature of life."

"I can believe that." Nile fidgeted with the braided tip of her ponytail, but appeared unconvinced. "With all that's happened I don't even want to think of what else there could be."

Mick left her side of the desk and went to hug her sister. "Me either Honey," she said, "me either."

***

Pike saw no need to pretend he was just some trustworthy houseguest who would wait patiently for his hostess to return from doing a good deed for her across-the-hall neighbor. He waited until Belle had been gone a good five minutes then commenced to easing his curiosity about what she kept in her cabinets and closets.

He grimaced frequently during his inspection of the kitchen cabinets. He hadn't dared to snoop when he was in there earlier for Rachel's water. He noted that Belle hardly kept a thing in there- a few cans of soup, an array of spices... the fridge was no better, though that could have been because she spent so much time on the road.

Pike wasn't buying it. She was practically starving herself. Smothering an oath- several oaths- he slammed the refrigerator door and headed for the back of the apartment.

The place radiated a coziness which didn't surprise him. She'd always had a knack for creating warmth in the most dismal spaces. He smiled, remembering the matchbox flat she had in Paris when she attended design school there.

The grimace returned to shadow his deeply bronzed face. He wouldn't allow himself to dwell on the time he'd spent there with her. Instead, he focused on his inspection of the bathroom.

Obviously feminine, he surmised as his dark eyes scanned the room in a cursory manner that missed nothing. The toilet seat was down as it should be- good. No condoms in the medicine cabinet- better. No birth control pills either. He smiled again. Her being on birth control would definitely put the kybosh on his plans to get her pregnant.

The thought gave him pause. If things hadn't gone as they had, they'd already be raising at least one child with another on the way. Their lives had been so busy before… but; as they'd both come from big families, he was sure they were on the same wavelength about kids. Hindsight was twenty/twenty. He thought of all the times they could have started the discussion and perhaps started the family. How many nights had he kept himself awake wondering whether she would have left if there had been a child between them?

Pike blinked out of that train of thought and became fixed on a familiar looking bottle in the medicine cabinet. Jaw clenched, he reached for the transparent caramel colored cylinder and shook the capsules filling it. Lightly, his thumb brushed the raised lettering on the label. He

A Lover's Shame

leaned against the counter and debated for all of ten seconds.

Reaching for his cell, he keyed the necessary digits and waited for the connection.

"Yes, good afternoon. Isak Tesano for Doctor Ewan Breneman."

TWELVE

"She really didn't do much damage. I just reinforced the seam." Belle explained about the prom dress she'd just finished repairing. "The stitching should hold, but let Kelly try it when she gets home and if anything else goes wrong," she jotted a name and number to the notepad on the coffee table, "she's a local seamstress. You can trust her with any other alterations."

Rachel clutched the pad to her breast and appeared to be uttering a prayer. "I can't thank you enough for this Belle and please forgive me for interrupting you and your

friend- Pike." Color fanned out in her cheeks when she
spoke the name.

Belle shook her head and decided to ease the
woman's curiosity.

"He's my ex-husband, Rache."

Rachel settled back on the lounge she occupied.
"Ex? I never would've guessed that."

"Well... he doesn't really look like the marrying
kind, I guess..."

"That's not it." Rachel's denial was instant. "He
looked completely infatuated with you- hardly took his
eyes off you the whole time I was there." She tilted her
head thoughtfully. "I'm guessing it was *you* who ended
things?"

Belle's vibrant brown stare narrowed
appreciatively. "You don't miss a thing. I can see why
you're an English teacher."

Rachel offered a flip shrug but she was obviously
quite pleased by the comment. The contentment didn't last
long though and soon she was leaning over to pat Sabella's
knee. "I shouldn't have pried."

"No, it's okay. I um... I did go after the divorce-
wasn't because I didn't love him." She braced her elbows
to her knees and bowed her head. "Rachel can you
understand how something even out of the vicinity of left
field could splat down on two unsuspecting people and
shatter everything between them?"

Rachel nodded somberly, thinking of her own failed
marriage. "You know, I'm probably the last person to

believe this and it's corny as hell to say it but would you buy that *sometimes* love conquers all?"

Belle laughed until moisture glistened in her stare. "I'll buy it." She scooted close for the hug Rachel offered.

"Thanks for speaking with me Doctor."

"Not a problem Mr. Tesano. Ms. Ramsey has you listed as next of kin in the event of an emergency. I believe it was a reflex action on her part, doubt she ever realized it was *your* name she gave but she never asked me to change it."

Pike tugged at the whiskers shadowing his jaw and took a moment to process the information.

"At any rate Doctor, I know there's not much you can tell me about what you're treating her for. I only want to know about the side effects of the medicine you've prescribed." Pike shifted on the arm of the sofa and switched the phone to his other ear. "I've tried hunting it down in the PDR and can't find anything."

"Well that doesn't surprise me. It's still in the development stages."

"Excuse me?"

"The drug isn't registered there yet."

"You're giving her something not even cleared for the market?"

"The prescription is filled privately, Mr. Tesano. Many of my patients are quite protective of their privacy. They aren't the sort who'd want to be picking up their medications at the local pharmacy."

"Why does she need it?"

"Mr. Tesano," Dr. Breneman's quick laugh harbored on uneasiness. "I'm sure you understand doctor patient privilege."

Pike smiled. "Either tell me what I want to know or find a padlock on your clinic before the day's done."

"Now just who the hell do you think you are? You can't just-"

"I can doctor. I promise you I can." Pike's tone sounded more vicious in its softness. "I'm not someone you want to screw with. Finding a padlock on your clinic door will be a lot less painful than a visit from me."

Breneman gasped. "Is that- is that a threat?"

"It's whatever you want it to be. Now do I make a few calls to shut down your practice and eventually turn your license into a worthless piece of paper or do you answer my question?"

"The medication is to treat panic attacks."

Pike settled to the sofa and propped his feet on the coffee table. "Go on."

"Presently there is no actual cure for them." The doctor explained in firm, clipped tones. "What triggers the attack manifests differently in each patient. Many live their lives in terror never knowing when one may strike or how powerful it may be."

"Powerful?"

"For some it's uncontrollable- shaking, crying, shortness of breath. For others… the attacks can take on violent tendencies."

Pike massaged the bridge of his nose. "How did Ms. Ramsey's attacks manifest?"

"I never really witnessed her in the throes of one. From what she's described I'm confident they were on the more violent side."

"Fuck..." Pike's grip on the phone threatened to crush it. "What are the side effects of this shit?"

Dr. Breneman cleared his throat, offended by the slight on his work. "The prescription has worked wonders for her bouts with the attacks. As long as she follows the regiment, I'm confident we can stifle the occurrences all together."

"And if she doesn't 'follow the regiment'?"

Again, the doctor cleared his throat. He gave no reply.

"Perhaps you'd feel better discussing this in person?" Pike suggested.

"I can't be sure of the reaction. Mr. Tesano you must understand this drug is still being developed-"

"I'll be there in twenty minutes doctor."

"Alright! Alright..." Breneman's sigh didn't reflect relief. "If she doesn't follow the regiment there is the risk of an episode so violent she could..."

"Could?"

"She could go into cardiac arrest. Mr. Tesano you *do* understand that *any* drug, if taken improperly, could result in death?" Breneman reasoned quickly.

"I'm glad you're aware of that, doctor." Pike's lashes fluttered slow as he fought to quell the darkness clouding his mind. "It'll save me the trouble of having to bring it up when I pay you a visit if anything happens to her."

***

Otto Fusilli's bald head appeared as red as his face when he saw his boss leaving the elevator. "Sorry boss," his eyes were wide and fearful. "They just walked in like they owned the place."

"It's alright Otto." Brogue laid a hand to the man's shoulder. "Bess already told me they were here."

"Who are they, boss?"

Brogue's light gaze rested on the heavy door to the cell where Marcus Ramsey lay in chains. "I've got a pretty good idea." He said.

The doors opened and three people- two men and one woman exited the chamber. The grim-faced trio was decked out in crisp suits and carried identical black valises. None of them offered a nod of greeting or made eye contact as they side stepped Brogue and Otto on their way down the tight fluorescent lit corridor.

"Who are they, boss?" Otto tried to lower his booming voice to a whisper. "You want me to stop 'em?"

"No." Brogue's voice was a whisper as well. He left Otto and went to look in on Marcus. The man lay in his usual spot, his body jerked as he slumbered restlessly.

Otto had come to peer across Brogue's shoulder and into the room. "What'd they do to him, boss? They weren't in there but a few minutes."

"No idea." Brogue shook his head. His face was a picture of bewilderment.

***

"I would've expected you to be more upset over this."

Quest smirked but the left dimple flashed for only a second. "I was plenty upset when Drake told me, but then Hill all but told me what he planned on doing."

Taurus tossed back another swig of the Heineken he balanced on one knee. "Guess I don't need to ask what Hill Tesano wants with stock from the weapons division but I'm still surprised you're so cool about it."

Quest rolled the 8 ball across the pool table and watched it break the others. "I didn't get the impression that he was up to no good."

"He just wants his brothers to *think* he is?"

Quest shrugged. "Some folks have different ways of doing the right thing and ...as Hill's never done the right thing..."

"Smoak and Pike would just think he's full of shit." Taurus finished. "You got any hints about what the fool's up to?"

"In Chicago, he told me he and Caiphus were working to bring it all down."

"His family?"

Quest shrugged, tugging on the cuff of the charcoal dress shirt hanging outside black trousers. "That's what I thought at the time."

"But now you're not so sure?"

Again, the left dimple flashed at Quest's smirk. "Hill likes for people to believe he's some big slab of muscle- not much brain so he'll be underestimated and can't be seen coming."

"Smart." Taurus let his head fall back to the armchair.

"Yeah…my guess is Hill came to see me for two reasons: he wanted to prove to himself that I was serious about not continuing what Marc and Houston had set down and to feed me that crap about bringing down his family which, while true, ain't even the half of it."

***

Outside Rye, New Hampshire~

"Rome…"

Roman sighed and looked over at his brother. Somber, knowing intensity filtered the probing depths of his eyes. "For the last time, I'm sure." He said.

Pitch weighed his keys against his palm. "You won't like what you find. I can promise you that. I've hardly scratched through the surface of it and I don't like it. It has literally freaked the hell out of me."

The admission gave Roman pause as there was very little that unnerved his older brother. What he saw in Pitch's eyes then went past being 'freaked the hell out'. The man was very much disturbed.

Roman reached across the gear shift and squeezed Pitch's hand. "Do you really think I'm gonna turn back now and let you keep carryin' this shit on your own?"

AlTonya Washington

After a short while, Pitch nodded and followed the gesture with a fist thump to Roman's chest. He smiled when Roman feigned discomfort. Silently, they left his gray Chevy Half Ton.

They were somewhere in New Hampshire but Roman had lost track of signs and turn offs the longer Pitch drove. His brother's love for The Moody Blues added a bit more eeriness to the drive especially when the group's classic *"Knights in White Satin"* drifted in through the speakers.

Now; as they headed across a creaky wooden walkway over a shallow stream, Roman felt a bit more of the unease. The house they approached could have been quite cozy from its lofty perch overlooking a vast forest not far from the Atlantic. Roman didn't expect this would be a 'cozy' visit.

Pitch knocked and then turned his back on the door and settled both hands into his suede jacket's pockets while they waited.

Roman had never felt more like the little brother than he did standing there on the small porch. All he wanted was to ask just one of the million questions racing his mind. Thankfully, the wait outside the peeling white wooden door didn't last very long.

The woman who answered appeared…disheveled but the square-framed spectacles perched on the tip of her nose lent her a somewhat scholarly appearance. Small, yet piercing dark eyes peered past the frames. They seemed to sparkle when they set upon Pitch.

"Well..." The sparkle melded with curiosity. "I would've put on a better robe had I known two dark handsomes would be visiting me today."

"Maddie," Pitch leaned way down to kiss the woman's cheek. "Doctor Madelyn Ferrat, my brother Roman."

Roman extended his hand which Madelyn pressed to her chest. She seemed content with keeping it there.

"Maddie? Hon, this is the married one." Pitch explained when Roman sent him a baleful look.

Madelyn gave a start. "The married one...*Roman*- yes, yes... You married the girl from Mozambique."

Alert then, Roman's sharpened gaze shifted to meet his brother's knowing one.

"That's right, Maddie." Pitch gave an encouraging nod. "Roman wants to hear the story you told me."

Madelyn laughed suddenly which tossed the wild sentry colored locks that fanned out over her head. Roman thought he could see traces of the young playful girl she may have once been before the years weathered her skin.

She gave a prissy wave and wrinkled her tiny nose. "He's not interested in that- just ramblings from an old crackpot."

"We don't think that Maddie. Neither do you."

Madelyn's playfulness vanished to be replaced by a frostier element. "Damn right," she raised her chin toward Pitch and regarded Roman with a keener more skeptical eye. "Are you sure you want to get into this, love?"

"I believe I'm already into it." Roman folded his arms over the quarter length denim jacket he sported.

"Hmph," Madelyn's eyes roamed his face appreciatively. "You're not even close to it and you'll think your brother an idiot for even listening to it." She spared Pitch a look before stepping closer to Roman. "By the way, I didn't track him down. He found *me*. I came here hoping to forget what I know- and I know surprisingly little."

Pitch laid a hand to the woman's bony shoulder. "We want to hear it anyway, hon."

Madelyn sized up the two men filling her doorway and finally shrugged. "What the hell…an old spinster like me should be giddy as a school girl having two sexy Italians paying her a visit and on the same day besides." She took Roman's arm when he crossed the threshold first. She looked up at him, winked and crushed her barely there breasts into his elbow.

"Did your brother tell you what happened the first time he came to see me? I wouldn't share my story until he made love to me."

Roman smiled. On the brink of laughter he sent Pitch a playful look.

Lies, Pitch mouthed the word.

"Lies, you say?" Madelyn challenged and nudged Roman's elbow again. "I'm a small woman, as you can see. Your brother's… affections definitely took their toll. You kept me in bed all that first day, didn't you Pitch? Tea, Roman?"

A Lover's Shame

"Uh," Roman smoothed a hand over his mouth and worked to stifle his laughter. "Yes, thanks a lot."

Pitch grabbed the sleeve of Roman's jacket to hold him back while Madelyn moved on. "The woman's lying Rome, I swear it."

Roman simply released his laughter and headed on towards Dr. Madelyn Ferrat's parlor.

THIRTEEN

"Isak?" Belle was calling out when she returned to her apartment from Rachel Hopman's. He wasn't in the living room so she went about replacing her sewing things in the front closet. When she turned around, he was right there behind her.

Belle took a moment to catch her breath. "I'm sorry for putting us so far behind."

"Don't worry yourself about that- we're good."

"So is it close? Where we're going?"

"More or less." The softness of his voice belied the piercing of his gaze. He watched as she began to wring her hands. "Why's it so important for you to know?" She was probably concerned about being too far away from that quack doctor of hers, he thought.

"Brogue's been talking to my mother…" She knocked her fist against her jaw and gave in to the worry that could no longer be ignored.

Taking pity, Pike sat on the back of the sofa and regretted his train of thought.

"With Marcus there with him- in that horrible place and… in that condition."

"Are you worried for your uncle?"

"If I was worried I would've already called my cousins."

Pike hid his smile and wondered if she realized the quickness with which she answered.

"Isak… Can I ask you something?"

"You can ask me anything."

She hesitated, preferring to walk the perimeter of the room for a minute or two. "Isak did Brogue say anything about why Marcus is there?"

Pike's smile reflected no humor then. "He's there because your mother put him there."

"Why?" She breathed the word. Having suspected as much, it was still a jolt to have those suspicions confirmed.

Pike's smile remained. "Why indeed…" he left the back of the sofa and came to stand before her. "Brogue says she hates him. Any idea why?"

Sabella's laughter was shaky at best. "Everybody hates him!"

"But the things Brogue says she's done to him. Had his people do to him- that's a special kind of hate." He tilted his head, awed by the emotions playing across her plump pecan brown face.

"He's a terrible man," she swallowed with great effort and brought her fingers to her mouth. "He…he makes people do terrible things- things they experience more shame over than he ever could."

Pike cupped her chin and blinked over the discovery of how badly she was shaking. "Bella, look at me. Look at me." He waited with admirable patience until she obliged. "The blame lies at *his* feet. Remember that," he nudged her chin, "remember that."

Belle opened her mouth to speak, but failed.

Pity and regret reasserted themselves and Pike pulled her to him. He kept his hand about her neck and kissed her deeply in an effort to soothe her nerves and quell his anger over what she was going through.

It worked for a time. Belle dropped her defenses and let the effects of the kiss claim her. She wasn't shy about touching as much of Pike as she could. She clutched the open collar of his shirt and whimpered while rubbing her tongue over and under his. She whispered his name while arching herself deeper into his frame.

Unfortunately, the shaking got the better of her and within minutes, she was bracing against him.

"Isak…" her whisper carried an edge that time. "Isak," she wrenched away unable to meet his gaze. "I'm sorry- sorry."

"Bella," Pike watched her dash toward the back of the apartment (where she kept her pills). "Bella!" He had a mind to follow her, but stopped himself. Torn between doing what was best for her and letting her have what she needed, he knocked his fist against the wall and bowed his head to pray for calm.

* * *

Over tea and angel food cakes cut into squares, Roman and Pitch listened to Madelyn Ferrat discuss her past scientific endeavors.

"…and then I went to work for a local gynecologist out of Portland. It was my hometown." She took a sip of the flavorful blueberry tea. "I decided to come back after college. In my day a young lady- even a very educated one- didn't venture too far away from home unless she was following a husband."

Roman and Pitch nodded politely. Roman nodded- Pitch was more interested in wolfing down the soft cakes.

"Then one day, the gynecologist I worked for had a visit from a young man. He was very handsome and I figured he was Italian given the olive tone of his skin, black hair and eyes and that soft musical voice and- oh my…" Madelyn's smile was suddenly bashful as though she'd realized her train of thought. "I *do* tend to get carried away," she said to Roman, "Italian men do that to me."

"Maddie… Be good," Pitch warned around a mouthful of cake.

"Of course," she helped herself to another sip of the tea and studied the contents of the cup before she spoke. "Well whatever the young man came for, he didn't get it. Left looking very put out, as I recall." She tapped a finger to her chin. "I also recall Doctor Cage, the gynecologist, making a remark about the nerve of the rich. He said, there was nothing scarier than a crazy man with enough money to fulfill his crazy ideas."

"Did you ever find out what he wanted?" Roman asked.

Again, Madelyn studied the contents of her cup. "To an extent…I went to work for him shortly after that. You see, I'd had enough of playing it safe- assisting old Doctor Cage with child births and physicals. Something about that young man and the mystery of what he wanted…"

"Maddie, tell Roman what he wanted." Pitch urged in a quiet tone.

Madelyn blinked as if she suddenly recalled that she hadn't included that bit of information. "Why he wanted ovaries, love."

The horror of Roman's expression equaled the chilling calm of Pitch's.

"What the hell for?" Roman asked.

Madelyn shrugged. "When we went to work for him-"

"We?"

"There were many of us young doctors and scientists in the area- we all wanted to work on something worthwhile." Madelyn reclined in the worn yet comfortable looking armchair and worried the collar of her floral housedress. Her gaze was riveted across the room as though she was looking into her past. "I think we were unceremoniously shown the door before we could make a break through into whatever the chap was after."

Roman braced his elbows to his knees. "What'd he have you doing with the ovaries?"

"It was all very strange." Madelyn shook her head. Her gaze held its far-away tint. "He was interested in their make-up how they might *evolve*...I'm not sure that he ever gave us specifics. It was like he was waiting around to see what we'd discover. I guess he found another game in town because all of a sudden he decided to show us the door. Hmph." She sipped more of her tea.

"Who was he?" Roman asked and noticed Madelyn's quick look toward Pitch.

"There are seven of you, right? Seven brothers?" Madelyn's tone held an odd lilt.

Roman looked toward Pitch as well and then he too nodded.

"A brother who's passed on..."

"Humphrey. He was the oldest of us. He died of a heart attack in ninety-seven."

"And another before him- long before."

"Stone."

"Yes...Stone...and how did *he* die?"

"Car accident."

"Ah yes, yes that's what the family was told."

Roman finally lost his very remarkable stream of patience. "I've never been much for drawn out stories Maddie, why don't you just get to the friggin' point."

"Alright," Madelyn's blue eyes were void of all playful coyness then. The directness of her expression made her appear even younger and far more formidable. "Your brother Humphrey was the man I went to work for. There were two others Gabriel and Stone. Your brother Stone did not die in a car accident, he was killed- murdered by Gabriel on Humphrey's order."

"Jesus!" Roman left his chair.

Pitch raised a hand. "Hear her out, Rome."

"Fuck that, I'm leavin'." Roman nodded once towards Madelyn. "Thank you Doctor Ferrat for wasting my time," he glared down at Pitch. "You comin'? Or stickin' around for a little afternoon delight?" He didn't wait for an answer and was half way out of the parlor when her voice reached his ears.

"They tried to kill you for snooping because what you were looking into would have eventually led you to them!"

Roman stopped.

A Lover's Shame

"They tried to kill you but it was your lovely Imani who got the bad end of it, right?"

Roman pivoted, on his way to give Madelyn the 'bad end' of his temper, not easily quelled once it was stoked. Pitch stood, planting his considerable frame between his brother and the doctor.

"You keep her name out of your mouth." He growled across Pitch's shoulder.

Madelyn didn't appear threatened. "You swore you'd kill the man who put her in that chair, didn't you?"

The angry tension eased slowly from Roman's body. His gaze shifted to Pitch's face and remained there as he addressed Madelyn. "I told her I wouldn't go after the son of a bitch until she was well."

Madelyn scooted toward the coffee table and reached for one of her angel cakes. "Would you go after the son of a bitch at all if you knew he was your brother Gabriel?"

***

Montecatini Valdi Cecina- Italy~

Sabella didn't wait to be helped from the SUV that carried them from the airstrip to the palazzo. She jumped from the back seat and held onto the open rear door while looking out in wonder at the rolling expanse of green hills before her eyes.

The palazzo was a rain-washed stone construction which; despite its fortress-like appearance, captured the essence of warmth. Belle was utterly speechless, as her expressive gaze wandered the breadth of the dwelling that was nestled amongst the woods and set beneath a late evening purple-orange sky.

Absently, she smoothed her hands across the seat of her jeans and turned to Pike for explanation. He was already watching her as if he understood her amazement.

"My granddad bought this place for my parents when they got married."

Belle pursed her lips as though she were about to whistle. "Some wedding gift," she murmured and moved farther along the stone walkway while Pike spoke with the driver.

Candlelight flickered invitingly from the windows, adding more to the cozy appeal. Sabella hugged herself and took time to appreciate the bold mountain peaks jagging high behind the palazzo. She closed her eyes to inhale the crisp, fragrant air. The only thing that made it all seem even more incredible was Pike walking up behind her and slipping his arms about her waist. She let her head fall back to his shoulders and relished the contentment.

"It tends to get chilly up here so you'll probably see the fireplaces goin'. The caretakers don't miss a beat even though the place doesn't get used that much."

"God, I can't imagine why," Belle shook her head against his shoulder. "I guess your dad had you guys over here all the time when you were young, huh?"

"He talked about it," Pike closed his eyes then, loving the way her hair blew against his face. His thoughts were more focused on the feel of her in his arms. "He actually talked about it a lot." Pike grinned. "Showed us lots of pictures and said he'd held onto it for when his sons got married." His laugh was short, but tender, "I guess it was some kind of bribe to get us to settle down."

Belle laughed then too. "Guess you were the only one to fall for that." She said, getting caught up in the lightness of the moment before she could stop herself.

"I've never regretted it, Bella."

She stiffened when his voice rumbled through her with a different resonance. He turned her to face him.

"I should've brought you here before."

"Isak…" The pressure of tears made her frown.

"Don't." She winced when his gentle hold turned vice tight.

"For how long?" He gave her a jerk.

She blinked, causing a tear to slide unexpectedly along the length of her cheek. Pike grumbled a curse and was kissing her seconds later.

"Don't Belle, I'm sorry…" He murmured, all the while his tongue coaxed hers to entwine with his. The gentle coaxing quickly turned hungrier more demanding.

Kissing him was all she wanted to be doing there with such beauty surrounding them. Unconscious of the driver unloading their things, she rubbed her hands over his shoulders and returned the hunger in his kiss. Shameless and needy, she rubbed her breasts into his chest, shivering at the friction that stimulated her nipples.

The action sent a renewed string of curses from Pike's seductively sculpted mouth. His fingers were curving into the front of her snug fitting knit sweater. He had every intention of ripping the lavender garment off of her, when a throat cleared in the distance.

Soft laughter passed between the couple and they submitted to a few moments of embarrassment.

Pike trailed a thumb across his brow and faced the driver. "Mi dá un secondo, fará lei Tino?" Turning back to Belle, he straightened the sweater over her chest. "Go on in, you'll find our stuff already in the room. Take a left at the first floor landing, double doors to the right. I'll be up in a sec."

She smoothed the back of her hand across the glossy whiskers darkening his jaw. "Will you speak to me in Italian later or do you only do that for Tino?" She teased.

He outlined her lips with his thumb. His brilliant deep stare followed the movement. "Farei niente per lei in qualunque momento lei mi chiede, Bella."

Her vivid browns studied his mouth. "What does that mean?"

"I'd do anything for you anytime you ask me." He smirked when she blinked clearly stunned by the depth of the words.

Belle waited for him to release her and she headed for the house without further comment.

Following a brief yet slow stroll through the ruggedly beautiful dwelling, Belle followed Pike's instructions to the bedroom.

"Great," she puffed out her cheeks when she spotted the suitcases on the floor next to the bed. Deciding to get it over with, Belle reached for the smaller of the cases Sabra had shipped to her in Vancouver.

"Hmph," she smirked, shaking her head though not all that surprised by her cousin's daring clothing selections.

Thinking of Sabra, Belle realized she hadn't thought to call her or anyone else for that matter. She could only hope no one was panicking. She shrugged off the possibility forbidding her thoughts to drift back toward the worry she was feeling for her mother. Instead, she dug out her phone and dialed her cousin's number.

"Uh yeah, Lee Lee Arnold here."

Belle smiled at the soft, harried voice of Sabra's assistant. "Hey Lee. It's Belle. Is she in?"

"Belle... girl is she ever..." Lee Lee groaned. Having known her *boss* for over fifteen years, Lee Lee knew the phrase was in name only. Lee Lee was the only one amongst Sabra's massive staff who could argue with her and get away with it.

"Is she alright?" Belle asked.

"Physically-yes. Mentally... Honey mentally, she's a wreck."

Belle pushed the case aside and sat on the bed. "Business stuff?"

"If it is, I can't put *my* finger on it and I know this place better than my own backside." Lee Lee's sigh came through the phone line. "I'd swear it's a man, but she's not seeing anyone. Besides, no man could rile her as much as she's been riled the last few weeks."

By then, Sabella was tapping her fingers to her chin. Her thoughts were riveted on the man who could very easily send her cousin into a thoroughly *riled* state.

"Let me talk to her Lee and thanks for the warning."

"Sure thing."

There was a silence for about five seconds as Lee Lee put the call through.

"Where the hell are you?" Sabra's voice filtered the line next.

Belle rolled her eyes. "Long story."

"It better be, dammit. You were supposed to call me from the hotel in Portland. What the fuck is goin' on?"

"I'm still with Isak, Sabi."

"Oh." The admission brought Sabra down more than a little. "Um…oh."

"Yeah…"

"Well um…are you…"

"I know I'll explain later. I just wanted you to know that I'm fine."

"Mmm hmm…I'm guessing *fine* is an understatement."

Belle fell back on the bed and began to toy with her hair. "I don't know how this happened. All of a sudden he was there in Portland and now I'm here with him in Italy…"

"Italy?"

"Mmm… We just sort of fell back into… everything."

"Well Sweetie, that's easy when you love someone the way you two love each other."

Belle closed her eyes. "He can't love me."

"Whatever...I won't try for the millionth time to get you to tell me why you believe that or why you ever left the sexy fucker in the first place. All I'll say is that your love has come back, it's obviously meant to be and you'd be the biggest fool ever to walk away from it again."

"Does that go for you and Smoak?" Belle braced up on her elbow when she heard her cousin gasp. "Does he have something to do with this crazier than normal mood you're in?"

"Damn that Lee Lee," Sabra snarled. "Hmph. Looks like we've both got long stories to share when we see each other. So I guess we won't be discussing anything just now. Enjoy Pike and come back with a little cousin for me to spoil."

The gasp came from Belle's throat that time.

Sabra was quiet on the other end of the line for a moment and then voiced her third 'Oh' of the conversation.

"Sabi. I gotta go." Belle shut down the phone and leaned over to brace her elbows on her knees.

Pregnancy wasn't a possibility she'd even entertained in spite of all the love (unprotected love) she and Isak had made over the last several days. She wasn't on the pill. There was no need to be. She couldn't think of any man touching her besides Isak Tesano. Pregnancy was not a possibility she could *ever* entertain- not when her own uncle was the reason for her very existence.

AlTonya Washington

The thought fueled the bile at the back of her throat. Before nausea could get the better of her, Belle pushed off the bed and decided a shower would do her good. She remembered the clothes but waved them off. The task of making a selection, could definitely wait until after her shower.

FOURTEEN

It seemed the task of making a selection from her new wardrobe wouldn't be an issue at all. After the steamy, rejuvenating shower, Belle returned to the bedroom to find the luggage had been removed. A sheer, burgundy lounging robe was all that lay on her bed.

"Isak…" she murmured. Smiling, she picked up the delicate garment, appreciating the tailoring of the transparent creation.

It was a scandalous-looking, but well-made piece of attire. Despite Sabra's sometimes outrageous taste in clothes, she bought nothing but the best made items, Belle admitted.

"Ah what the hell..." She gave in. Setting aside the robe, she fixed the high ponytail she sported and then prepared to slip into her underwear.

"Panties..." she whispered, looking over the bed for a pair. "Panties?" Her heart began a slow ascent toward her throat. "Come on Isak...don't do this to me..." Belle knew she was wasting her time in continuing the search and finally consented to donning the sheer piece of nothing and *nothing* else.

Dressed, for what it was worth, she set out to find Pike. Her walk through the house that time was a lot slower and more attentive. Oversized sofas and cushiony chairs were spaced throughout the rooms on the lower level. Each room boasted a massive stone hearth that was ablaze with raging flames which made Belle shiver from contentment instead of cold.

She'd yet to set sight on Pike and didn't begin to frown until she reached the kitchen and found no sign of him anywhere. It was then that she heard the music and realized she could feel the dull bump of bass beneath her bare feet.

"Isak?" She didn't expect him to answer as she moved toward an open door at the rear of the kitchen.

A stairway greeted her there. Without care for her bare feet or the cool air nipping her skin through the thin robe, Belle headed down into the darkness. More inviting warmth greeted her once she met the landing and took the

A Lover's Shame

rest of the steps down. The music was louder- a mix of 90s conscious rap from Digible Planets had her humming familiar beats and softly mouthing a few lyrics as she reached the end of the narrow L-shaped stairway.

Her eyes took but a moment to adjust to the fluorescent lighting and her breath caught once she was finally able to focus on the area. It appeared the entire basement level of the palazzo- and more beyond that- had been turned into a state of the art garage.

Along one far wall of the concrete room waited a row of cars that could make any race car driver swoon. The line-up ranged from foreign model sports cars and sedans to top of the line SUVs and monster trucks.

The music silenced all of a sudden and Belle heard the wolf whistle echoing across the room. She turned, finding Pike leaning against the open hood of a sleek black Japanese Drift model. He tossed aside the paper towel he'd been using to dry his hands and folded his arms over his chest while smiling and nodding appreciatively.

"Well done Sabra." He said.

Belle let her gaze falter yet resisted the urge to purr in response to the deep, lazy drawl of his words.

"I remember putting my own underwear in those cases before we left Vancouver." She told him instead.

"You did," Pike bowed his head and focused on kicking a nearby tool chest with the toe of his hiking boot. "And if I thought you'd need any, I would've given them to you."

Belle simply pressed her lips together. She had no idea how to respond.

Pike's satisfied expression however merged with a touch of unease when another thought filtered his brain. "It's um…it's not that *time of the month,* is it?" His quiet voice was softer in the wake curiosity.

"No." Belle shook her head while her cheeks burned. Silently, she prayed there *would* be a 'time of the month' and soon.

"Are you cold?" His voice was still quiet as his ebony stare drifted down the length of her.

"Not right now." She scanned the garage again. "Whose idea was this?"

"Mine," he looked around as well. "I got interested in the whole Japanese Drifting thing when I was over there one year on business. Drifting's um," he used his hands to emphasize. "It's when you maneuver the car so that the tail end is out. The object is to keep it as far out as you can for as long as you can before realigning it smoothly…anyway, I was over there shortly after we…" He turned to look down into the hood of the car. "I got more and more interested in cars, what made 'em tick," his grin was somber. "I wanted to know what made 'em tick and *I* wanted to be the one to make 'em do it."

"Sounds exciting," Belle folded her arms beneath her breasts.

"Wasn't really thinking about the excitement of it," Absently, he smoothed a hand across sweat slicked abs visible behind his open denim shirt. The absent manner was reflected in the deep pools of his eyes. "I'd have taken up stamp collecting if it would have helped me forget you."

Belle was first to break eye contact when he looked at her. "I'll um…" she reached for the hem of her robe while turning, "just let you get back to work."

He caught her just as she reached the landing.

"Isak…"

He braced his forehead against hers and trapped her to the concrete wall. "I'm sorry if this is hard for you Bella but how long do you expect us to keep avoiding what happened like it's some bull in the room?"

"Nothing can come of it," she spoke in the same soft, tortured manner he did.

Pike's long lashes settled slowly as if he were drawing on some inner strength to quell his rage before it had the chance to ignite. "How can you say that?" He spoke eventually. His voice was slow, controlled.

She inhaled the scent of him, cherishing their closeness in spite of the tension. "It's best to leave it the way it is."

"And what way is that?" He pulled back to glare down at her. "You wallowing in shame and misery?" He pretended not to notice the way her eyes flashed to his face. "Or me tryin' to figure out why the hell you walked away without giving me the chance to help you through it?"

She shook her head. "You don't know what you're saying," her pecan brown face was a study in bewilderment. "There is no *help* for this."

"Alright," he ground down fiercely on his jaw and caused the muscle there to dance. "But know this Bella, there is nothing," he wrapped his hand about her neck and made her look at him.

"*Nothing* you can tell me that'll change the way I feel and you know how I feel, don't you?" He tilted his head, encouraging her reply which she only gave in the form of a minute nod.

"You need to understand that I don't intend to let you leave me again," he spared a moment to grant her a grim smile. "I did that already. I played the nice guy- the idiot. I made myself let you go- told myself not to hold you if you didn't want to be held. I tried so hard not to give into that…that side that told me to play dirty and ruthless as hell to keep you. I didn't give into that and I wound up losing you for seven years." He shook his head once. "I can't let you walk away from me again."

Belle's cheeks glistened with the tears that streamed from her eyes in a steady progression. "Isak I'm sorry for ruining what we had but what happened…" her breathing was choppy as the emotions welled up relentlessly. "I never saw it coming and I can't go back and change it and God how I wish I could change it. How I so wish I could erase everything about that day- everything except the time I had with you. I wish I'd let you ditch that meeting…"

"Bella…" he squeezed his eyes shut tight, remembering the day she spoke of.

She ran the back of her hand across his face. "I wish we'd just kept on driving…" she nuzzled his nose with hers. Her mouth parted for a kiss but she resisted the urge.

"It's just not possible to go back and I-I hate myself for what I did to you. You were so good, so sweet and I damaged that. I turned you into someone hard and angry. Of all the things I have to be ashamed of, I'm most ashamed of what I did to you." She could scarcely see him through the water blurring her eyes.

"Tell me why you left." He leaned closer and spoke the words against her cheek. He felt her shake her head, refusing the question. His jaw muscle flexed again as the dark depths of his gaze smoldered with renewed frustration.

"Do you understand that *not* telling me won't keep me away any more than telling me?"

Irritably, Belle set her head back against the wall. "Isak let me go."

"No way in hell. You're never getting rid of me again. A stalker wouldn't have a thing on me Belle. I'd be that and more. I won't give you a minute's peace- not anymore."

"Isak-"

"Do you know why?" Again, he cupped her neck and commanded her eyes to his. "Do you love me?"

"Yes." She didn't hesitate to breathe the word.

His smile then, belied the intensity lurking in his black stare. "That's why," he said just seconds before his mouth claimed hers.

The effect on Belle was instant, as usual. She held nothing back and kissed him with love, abandon, regret and desperation all equally mixed. Murmuring helpless whimpers, she let his tongue overpower hers, while claiming dominance during the kiss. He gave her little time to catch her breath, but she didn't care. She wanted whatever he had to give in whatever manner he saw fit to give it.

She stood on her toes and encouraged him with soft taunts urging him not to stop and to give her more. Her nails raked the carved expanse of his copper toned chest that was partially visible beneath the dingy denim shirt that hung open outside a pair of equally grimy sagging jeans. She could feel the growl simmering in his chest and she shivered at the sensations it set loose inside her. His kiss was as punishing as it was passionate. His whiskers branded her skin each time he tilted his head in a new direction.

Roughly, Pike grasped the robe, tugging the sheer material higher along the lush length of her leg.

"Isak, mmm…" her voice was wavery at best. Her hand roamed the curve of a broad shoulder, about the nape of his neck and her fingers sank into the thick darkness of his hair.

Pike took advantage of her upswept ponytail. He broke the kiss to slide his mouth along the graceful line of her neck. He took care to nip at a few stray chestnut brown tendrils that curled against her ear. His hand had

A Lover's Shame

disappeared beneath the robe's transparent burgundy material and began to explore.

Pure arrogance could only describe the smile tugging at his lips when she emitted a small needy sound as his fingers probed her heat. Immediately, she began to move in sync to the intimate caress. Her lips parted to moan as her head pressed back into the wall. Changing her mind, she moved forward to bury her face in his neck and lost herself among waves of sensation.

Belle pleaded with him to do more, knowing Pike was the only one who could satisfy what screamed inside her to be fulfilled. Emboldened, she curved her hand over the pronounced bulge straining his button fly. The overt power and the pleasure the organ promised merely compounded her eagerness. She plied his neck with wet kisses and worked to undo his jeans.

Pike could feel strength leaving his legs as he let her free him. When she took him in her hand, whatever strength he had left, became a distant memory. All that remained was a hunger.

In one effortless, sexy move he lifted her high against the wall and claimed her. He watched the range of emotions play out on her exquisite dark face. His ego was as completely stroked as the rest of him by the bliss in her expression and the knowledge that he was responsible for it. His gorgeous bronzed face rested against her chest, until he'd managed to work his way past the robe's scant material.

Belle could scarcely catch her breath. Isak filled her that thoroughly, stretching her walls anew with every thrust he treated her to. His mouth felt like perfection against her breasts. He lathered her nipples with generous wet strokes, and then outlined the rigid buds for a few erotic moments. Afterwards, he subjected them to merciless suckling keeping in sync to every lunge of his sex inside hers.

Thanks to the height advantage offered by her present position, Belle indulged in the rare treat of burying her face in his hair and luxuriating in its mink texture.

Pike took her rigorously and over a lengthy stretch of time against the wall. He groaned her name constantly, clutching her ever more tightly. His big hands were an excellent cradle for her ample bottom.

"I can't wait," he spoke harshly into her chest after the longest time.

"Don't…" she urged, having reached the limits of her restraint as well.

Dual sounds of satisfaction filled the small area of the landing. Belle purposefully clenched herself about his shaft when she felt the fluid warmth of his seed. The pleasure of his desire spreading through her added yet another layer of stimuli to an already amazing orgasm.

Pike was almost completely spent. He braced one hand to the wall, the other kept Belle's thigh raised near his hip. His forehead dropped to her shoulder where he made a valiant attempt at catching his breath.

A Lover's Shame

Moments later, they'd slid down the length of the wall. Cradling one another, they eased into a heavy slumber.

The rest; not to mention previous actions, should have gone far in easing tensions. Belle woke feeling like her nerves were on fire. She'd been sleeping on Pike's chest. Squeezing her eyes shut, she willed herself back to sleep wanting to return to wherever her dreams had taken her as she slumbered. She inhaled the scent of oil, sweat and soap clinging to Pike's skin and creating some sort of intoxicating unmistakably masculine fragrance that was an aphrodisiac all its own.

Her nerves felt like they were on fire.

Belle raised her head, looking down at Isak as he slept. Gently, she ran her fingers across his wide brow and then she noticed her hand. It was shaking.

"No." She clenched a fist. "Please," she whispered as though begging would stop what was coming.

Slowly, she unclenched her fist. The shaking had intensified. With purpose then, she pushed herself up from the landing and began a frantic ascent up the staircase. She stumbled over the robe's flowing hem and gathered some of the material in one trembling hand. She grasped the wooden bannister in the other.

The commotion roused Isak. He woke up frowning but came alert when he realized she wasn't there next to him. Soon, he was ascending the staircase as well.

Belle ran to the bedroom in search of her purse. She prayed Pike hadn't taken it when he'd moved the suitcases. She found it in an armchair. Her heart pounded and she fell to her knees bracing against the seat of the chair while taking only a few seconds to catch her breath. Then she was back to the task of tearing apart her tote bag.

"Where is it?" She dumped the contents of the tote to the carpet. She spread her hands over every possession, but the pill bottle was not among them.

A frustrated gurgling sound had found a place in her throat and settled there. Belle curled her fingers into her unraveling ponytail and scanned the room with wide, frightened eyes. Her gaze shifted toward the bathroom.

Stumbling again; when she tripped over the robe, she scurried to her feet. She sprinted for the bath where she hoped to find her prescription.

The medicine cabinet was empty of course and that gurgling sound of frustration became a full-fledged scream. Belle slammed the cabinet door with vicious intensity, oblivious to the glass shattering and sending shards across the counter and floor. Defeated, she stood there clutching the rim of the sink. Her head was bowed as she submitted to the horrendous shaking which had taken hold.

The knocking caught her ear and she turned to find Pike leaning against the doorway. In his hand, was the bottle she wanted.

"Is this what you're looking for?" He asked.

A Lover's Shame

FIFTEEN

"Give it to me."

"Why'd you start taking them?"

"Give them to me, Isak."

"Tell me why you started-"

"I told you-"

"Yeah, you did. This time I want you to tell me the truth."

Belle ran her hands through the hair spilling across her shoulders. "I told you the truth."

"Right. Your job is stressful. Tell me the rest."

The shaking was getting the better of her. Her nerve endings fired, sending frenzied messages to her brain.

"Isak, please. *Please*." She clutched his open shirt and tugged his sleeve in hopes of getting him to lower his hand. "Isak…"

He simply held the bottle out of her reach. "Tell me the rest."

She pounded his chest then, smirking when she managed to unsettle his stance just a bit. "You give them to me. You have no right."

"Tell me the rest."

"Dammit, what rest?!"

"Tell me about Marcus!"

Belle jerked away from Pike as if he was suddenly burning hot to touch. "What did you say?" Her radiant brown stare narrowed in disbelief.

"You found out about Marcus, didn't you?"

She shook her head, looking nervously from side to side as she retreated into the bathroom.

"You found out what happened. What he did to your mother."

"You shut your mouth!" She closed her eyes and turned her back on him.

Pike's features reflected distress and concern. He couldn't stop, not that time. It was the reason he'd brought her there. They wouldn't avoid this conversation not after all that had happened- not now.

"You know he raped her. Somehow you know."

"God…" she moaned, squeezing her eyes shut then as she went to her knees. Huddled next to the counter, she bowed her head and folded her fingers over the rim of the sink. "You can't know that. Oh God…you can't ever know that…"

The pitiful, childlike sound of her voice broke his heart. He wanted to go to her, but a glance at the prescription bottle, stopped him. There was more to be said. There was more he needed to know.

"Marc told me. Honey, he told me the day I went out to Brogue's- the day you came to stop me." He took a tentative step past the doorway. "That's what happened the day I left you at Carmen's. Did she tell you?"

"You can't know, you can't…" Belle was still moaning, rocking herself in an awkward manner as she sat on her knees near the cabinet.

"Babe…" He dropped down beside her, needing to console her, to give her what strength he had. "Baby none of it matters. I love you. Let me take care of you-"

"I don't want your pity!" She wrenched away from him and scooted back to brace on her hands and knees. "What do you know about it?! What the hell do you know about what *matters*?!" The second her eyes locked on his, the anger vanished replaced once again by anguish and shame. She'd lived with the emotions so long they'd carried their own unhealthy spot in her soul.

She wrapped her arms about her stomach and doubled over. The moaning was fainter- resembling more of a mewling as though she were winding down. "I left so you wouldn't know- don't you see?" She lifted her head a bit. "Don't you see that Isak? I didn't want you dirty-dirty... dirty like me..." She pressed her forehead to the tiled floor.

"Honey..." He slid across the floor, gathering her in his arms and settling her back against him. He pulled her hair from the robe's collar and kissed her neck. "Belle I love you. I love you-it's got nothing to do with pity. Let me help you, let me..."

She was shuddering terribly, but had stopped resisting his closeness. Her eyes were closed and; blindly, she reached for his shoulder and squeezed.

"I'm not goin' anywhere," he kissed her temple when she squeezed his forearm.

Belle closed her hand over his. Before Pike could react, her nails were scratching at his fingers which were still curved around the bottle.

"Belle? Bella." He knew she couldn't hear him. Her sole focus was on the drug she thought she needed.

"Belle no," he wrenched her hand away from his.

She slapped him, smiling eerily once the contact was made. She moved in for another strike, but he captured both her wrists easily in his hand.

"I hate you!" She moved wildly against him.

Pike kept hold of her. He forced her to her feet and pulled her across the bathroom where he popped the cap on the pill bottle. When Belle saw that he meant to pour the contents into the toilet, she struggled for all she was worth.

"No! Isak, no!" She pushed at his chest, intent on moving him back from the toilet.

Pike was immovable, but Belle at last succeeded in wrenching herself from his hold. Her dark and lovely features had taken on a disturbed glean. Her fists clenched and her wild glare was set on him before her eyes moved toward one of the glass shards littering the counter.

"Isak? Put it down, Isak."

Pike did a double take when he saw her brandishing the shard as a weapon- a weapon she was unconsciously digging into her own flesh.

"Bella..." He dropped the bottle and raised his hands. Quietly, he prayed, hoping she'd charge toward him and not use the glass piece on herself.

"Baby...shh...Honey hear me, hear me, it's okay... it's Isak, you're alright..."

Belle gazed warily at his raised hands and kept the shard extended. She hurried to the toilet, dropping to her knees beside it. She slapped her hand around in the water, trying to catch the stray pills floating there.

Pike couldn't move, helpless to do anything other than stand and study her in awe. He was as horrified by her actions as he was by fear for her and how a terrible discovery had not only shamed her, but was killing her.

He blinked as though he were suddenly coming to. The shard slipped from her bloodied hand seconds before she lost consciousness and slid to the floor.

***

As instructed, Brogue kept his staff light that evening. The atmosphere should have been appealing. Instead of silence, a Schubert arrangement colored the air with sometimes haunting, sometimes exuberant phrases that most would find inviting.

For Brogue, it made the atmosphere seem eerie. It was all he could do to keep turning the pages of the well-used *Hustler* magazine he thumbed through while leaning against the wall.

"How much longer do you think it'll be, boss?" Otto Fusili asked in a semi-hushed tone.

Brogue's vivid blue gaze slanted from the magazine and he smiled. "I'd say not much longer." He'd heard the faint ding of the elevator at the far end of the concrete corridor.

First out of the elevator, was the man who hired him followed by a group of rough looking sorts. Brogue didn't know them, but recognized them as characters most likely in the same business that he was.

Last off the elevator was Carmen Ramsey. The woman; lovely and fragile looking, should've appeared out of place in such grim and musty surroundings. She looked more at home than Jasper Stone and his team of henchmen.

Brogue was already heading toward the group. Smiles and pleasant greetings weren't necessary. He simply extended his hand, nodding when Jasper accepted the gesture.

"How's the guest?" Jasper asked.

Brogue glanced cross his shoulder at the thick double doors. "Better than he's been since he got here. Rested, fed…quiet."

"Back to his old self?" Carmen's light eyes were riveted on the door.

"Not even," Brogue felt himself cringe in response to the wicked smile curving the woman's exquisite honey toned face.

"You have what we asked for?" Jasper said once Carmen had walked on ahead.

"Containers are right past the door."

Jasper nodded once and clapped Brogue's shoulder. He tilted his head toward his men and followed them to the double doors.

Inside the dark chamber, Carmen was already hunched on the heels of her silver pumps next to where her brother sat chained against the wall. She tilted her head this way and that like a child observing some caged animal at a zoo.

"Marc? Marcuuus…" She drawled, tauntingly soft until he jerked from an uneasy sleep.

It took some time before he was lucid enough to recognize who called out to him, "Carm…Carmen please after all this time…please I promise-"

"Promise what, Marcus?" Carmen smiled, feigning pity when he remained silent. "What does it feel like to have nothing, not even a quick lie to make someone feel at ease before you pounce on them with all that evil you have inside you?"

"Carmen please…"

She moved suddenly and open-handed his face viciously. "Shh…" her voice still carried the sweetest of tones. "We don't have time for promises now anyway. I brought you a visitor- an old friend."

As the fluorescent lights illuminated the room, Jasper kneeled. He tilted Marc's head back and studied him much like a doctor would. "It's Jasper Stone, Marc."

"Jas-" Marc coughed but it did nothing to rid the hoarseness from his voice. "Jasper?"

"Guess I don't need to ask how you're doing?"

"Jasper…Jasper talk to her," Marcus' head lolled toward Carmen when Jasper released his face. "Tell her to let me out of here."

Jasper laughed. "Why would I do that when I put you here?"

Marcus whimpered, hands flexing above the shackles he wore. Understanding that his plight had worsened, he squeezed his eyes shut tight and let his head fall back to the wall.

"I honestly can't believe how well it all worked out." Jasper sat back on his haunches and let his arms dangle over jean-clad knees. "Do you remember the night I beat the hell out of you? Do you remember what I said? I promised you wouldn't survive what I'd have on tap?" He grinned. "Actually, I promised to do all that *after* Carmen told me what you'd done to her so…My apologies for not being able to wait that long. I hope you've been enjoying yourself here.

Sometimes fate does shine down favorably. When Carmen approached your host- oh, that would be Brogue Tesano." Jasper shared as though it were something Marc should have been aware of.

"She wanted him to help her take you- make you suffer. I'd say it was one of our young Mr. Tesano's easiest jobs since my plans were in the works for you to be here doing precisely that long before she came looking for help."

Carmen who was still kneeling next to Marcus, flashed a surprised glance in Jasper's direction but decided not to make a point of it just then.

"…all the people you've shitted on during the years. They finally came together with a common goal- to see that you paid and that it'd be the last thing you experienced in your pathetic life. Even Charlton got in on the deal." He referred to their old friend Charlton Browning a.k.a. Cufi Muhammad. Jasper shrugged. "Of course for him and his wife Yvonne, the payback was about money. It was more personal for Josephine and Johnelle Black." Jasper's smile deepened when he saw surprise flicker on Marc's battered face.

"Oh yes, your wife and that poor girl's mother were a great deal of help." Jasper's easy expression hardened into something dangerous and he tilted his head toward Carmen. "Now it's her turn."

Carmen stood and brushed her hands across the seat of her curve hugging black linen suit. "It's funny you should mention promises, Marc. I made one of my own long ago- that you'd burn." She reached for one of the heavy red gasoline containers that Jasper's men had placed nearby. She began to sprinkle the gas like she was casually watering a garden. She added more generous amounts to her brother's tattered clothing and the area surrounding him.

"Carm," Marc gasped, flinching with every drop of gasoline that touched his skin. "Carmen please! I'm sorry! God help me, I'm sorry! All these years- I learned my lesson after all these years! Can't you- Jesus, can't you be good enough to forgive me?!"

The words left Marc's lips a second before Jasper kicked him full across the mouth. Marcus would've fallen to the floor were it not for the chains binding him. He sat there awkwardly suspended. His head was slumped over as he tried to bring his hands to his mouth.

"There, there…" Carmen soothed even as she poured a healthy amount of gas over his head and watched as the liquid burned his eyes and the wounds Jasper had reopened with his kick.

Carmen blinked, stepping back to watch her brother scream and writhe in agony. He was literally crying when Jasper handed her a long-stemmed match. Carmen studied the stick and the rough rounded blue and purple tip where her justice resided.

"Dammit to hell," she whispered.

A Lover's Shame

"What?" Jasper crossed to her. "What's wrong?"

Carmen's laugh held no humor. "I wish you could tell me. Why can't I do this?" Her gaze was questioning as it searched his. "Why am I hesitating? I've thought of this ever since the night he…"

"Shh…" Jasper tugged her close, pressing a kiss to the soft hair pulled back from her face. "You're hesitating because you're a good person. As hard as you want hate and evil to consume you the way it has that piece of shit chained to the wall, it hasn't." He stepped back to look down into her face. "On top of all that very important, very true stuff, it's just not all that easy to take a life. Trust me, I know."

A quick knock echoed through the doors and Brogue stuck his head just inside. "Sorry for interrupting. Carmen, there's a call you need to take. It's Pike- it's about Belle."

"Belle?" Carmen forgot everything after the whisper of her daughter's name. She hurried toward Brogue. "Why's Isak calling? What's happened?"

Brogue moved to lay a reassuring hand to Carmen's shoulder, but chose to push that hand into his trouser pocket instead. "He wouldn't say. Told me to tell you that you could either take his call or if you wanted to duck him the way you've been ducking Belle, you could just sit here and imagine the worst."

"Where's the phone?" Carmen asked.

Brogue led the way to a beaten metal desk in the corner of the room.

Carmen studied the receiver for a moment before pressing it to her ear. "Isak?"

Jasper watched Carmen take the call. Every part of him wanted to be there close to her, helping her process whatever she was being told about her daughter- their daughter?

A curdled, unsettling sound caught his ear then. After several seconds, Jasper recognized it as laughter. It was laughter from the most surprising source.

Eyes closed and mouth glistening with fresh blood and gasoline, Marcus laughed weakly. "She won't do it," he wheezed. "She won't- she can't... No matter what happened. I'm family-" A bout of coughing interrupted him for a moment or so. "Blood- blood is thick, Jas. Thicker than the slime runnin' through *your* veins, brotha. Jasper Stone... son of a whore..."

Jasper was turning to face off with his sneering former friend when the echo of the phone receiver; hitting its cradle, filled the room.

Carmen braced against the desk. Head bowed, she appeared to be praying. Brogue side-stepped her when she turned to head in Jasper's direction. Just as she reached him, she veered off course, struck the long-stemmed match and let it fall.

Marc's sneer transformed into an expression of terror. He tried scurrying to his feet. The chains rattled the walls as he fought to avoid the flames that were closing in on all sides. Carmen moved into Jasper's arms and buried her face into his chest.

Marcus Ramsey's cries; high pitched, maddening and deafening, saturated the room as he met his death.

SIXTEEN

"¿Signore Tesano?"

Pike was sitting-leaning over with his elbows resting on his knees. He studied the mobile phone from which he'd placed the call to Carmen. He took time to consider what he'd just said to her and where things would go from there.

"¿Signore Tesano?"

The soft, melodic voice drifted in once more. Pike jumped to his feet. He dwarfed the smaller man, while gripping the lapel of the lab coat he wore.

"¿Sta bene?" *Is she alright?* He asked.

The doctor's kind, dark face softened further by the smile he offered. He waved toward the chair Pike had just leapt from. "Sediamo," he suggested they sit.

After a while, Pike obliged. He reclaimed his seat while the doctor took the one across from him. "¿Sta bene, il dottore?"

"She's fine." The doctor's smile broadened when he saw the relief spread on the younger man's face.

Pike put his head between his knees and clutched fistfuls of his hair. "Thank you God…"

The doctor leaned over to pat his shoulder and Pike looked up. Clearing his throat, he extended his hand.

"¿Dottore…?"

The man nodded. "Giorgi Bottazzi."

"Doctor Bottazzi, thank you. Thank you." Pike's dark eyes shifted past the man's shoulder. "Are you sure she's…"

"Senora Ramsey lost consciousness which was a blessing in her case. Had she gotten any more of the pills into her system, she could have very well gone into cardiac arrest."

Again, Pike hung his head and gave thanks. "May I see her, doctor?" He asked when he looked up again.

"Si," Dr. Bottazzi continued to smile. "She's very weak, I warn you. We'll want to keep her for a little while longer."

A Lover's Shame

Pike stood near the room door for long moments before daring to step forward. Nervously, he twisted the tails of his dingy shirt between his fingers. She looked so depleted, so completely worn out. His heart ached for her as though something had actually taken hold and was twisting it without mercy.

Belle shifted beneath the covers and Pike forgot about how upset he was. "Bella?" He took the hand that lay across her hip and squeezed to offer reassurance, security.

"I'm here Bella." He placed a ragged kiss to the back of her hand and waited, watching her turn her head into the direction of his voice.

With effort, Belle forced her eyes open. They filled with tears the moment she looked up and saw his face.

"I didn't mean it," her voice was barely a whisper. Frantically, she shook her head on the pillow. "I didn't mean it, Isak. I'm sorry...I'm so sorry, God..."

"Shh...stop. Bella? Stop." He ordered, and then simply smothered her apologies by bringing his mouth down on hers.

"You're never to apologize to me for this. Not one part of it." He folded his hand into her hair and held it close to her cheek. "Do you understand?"

"Isak..."

"Do you understand me, Bella?"

Resignedly, she let her lashes flutter down and nodded. "I have to tell you about that day." She kept her eyes closed.

Pike followed suit. "I don't need to hear-"

"Yes, you do. I owe you that." She brought her hand to his. "I owe you that." Belle waited for his nod which came very reluctantly. Satisfied, she tried to sit up.

"Wait-" he straightened suddenly and tried to assist her.

"I'm alright, I can-"

"Hush for a minute," he angled himself in behind her on the bed and secured her against his chest. "Alright?" He spoke next to her temple and smiled when she nodded.

"She was on the phone with my aunt Bri when I got there." Belle shuddered on the memory and clutched Pike's hand for support. "It didn't take long for me to realize the conversation wasn't a nice one but something in Mama's voice wouldn't let me move from the door. I listened and... then she just- she just...said it. She said what he did to her." Tears got the better of her then.

Pike buried his face in her hair but didn't try to silence her. He knew she needed to cry and probably would for a long time to come.

"I just stood there." She was clutching his arm then, her face tucked in the crook of his elbow. "I couldn't move- felt like I stood there for the longest time. I um...I managed to turn around and get out before she knew I was there."

"When I came back to pick you up, Carmen said she hadn't seen you." Pike ground the muscles in his jaw as memories of that day resurfaced for him as well. "I guess we talked for about a half hour before I called your cell to see if you'd stopped off somewhere else first. I didn't get

A Lover's Shame

worried when you didn't answer, but when I called a
second time and then a third…"

"I went to the beach." She said, smiling weakly
then. "Remember Mama's house is on that quiet street right
across from it?"

"Great sunsets," Pike recalled, smiling too as he
remembered the times they'd spent enjoying them during
previous visits to Carmen's.

"Yeah…" Belle sniffled and snuggled her head
deeper into his arm. "I sat out there for about two hours and
then I walked. I walked until my feet hurt and then I caught
one of the busses that ran along the strip. My phone kept
vibrating from all the missed calls. I got off at the first
hotel, checked in and stayed in the shower until the water
got too cold. I was trying- trying to wash off…" She hid
her face in his shirt.

"Babe…" Pike squeezed his eyes shut on the
sudden pressure of tears. He pressed a hard kiss to the top
of her head. "Why'd you shut me out? Why wouldn't you
let me go through it with you?"

"How do you think I could tell you something like
that?" She raised her head but didn't look up at him. "I
think I threw up every day the first three months after I
found out. I sickened myself. I couldn't tell you and watch
you be sickened by me too."

"Belle…"

She shook her head and scooted up a bit in his
embrace. "I wanted to have your babies, Isak. Lots of

them…we hadn't discussed it but I hoped once our jobs calmed down maybe…"

Pike let his tears show themselves then.

"How could I bring a child into the world not knowing if it'd be… because my uncle is my father?"

"Honey please…" He couldn't stand anymore. Besides, the familiar tingle of rage was starting to well up inside him. His hands itched with the need to choke the life from Marcus Ramsey's body. That need quelled when Belle squeezed his hand and he felt her tears wet his skin. He pushed her hair across her shoulder and spoke against the nape of her neck.

"Don't you know you're enough for me? You'll always be enough?"

"I never wanted you to have to settle for that. I wanted you free-free to find someone to give you what you deserve because you deserve the best."

Pike slipped out from behind her on the bed and sat on the edge to face her. "I *had* the best and I lost her. She's all I want."

Belle couldn't see him through the water in her eyes. She looked away but Pike followed by tilting his head to keep his eyes on her round, lovely face.

He moved closer outlining her generous mouth with the tip of his thumb. "The freedom you thought you were giving me Love… it wasn't freedom, it was hell."

"Isak," she pushed the thick blue-black tufts of hair from his face. "It could still be hell. I'm not the person you knew."

A Lover's Shame

"That's a lie. You're exactly the person I knew."
His gaze was every bit as flattering as his words. "I've
loved you since I met you and then it was because you were
so damned good to look at."

Belle couldn't mask her smile. She would have
brought her hand up to hide it had Pike not captured it
between both of his.

"And then I got to know you and who you were
inside was even more amazing." He shook his head and
fixed her with a helpless look. "There's no way for me to
explain it- no way to explain how you affect me Belle. Just
know that I can't survive losing you again. I can't survive
it. I love you."

She cried full and deep then. There were no breathy
sobs or sighs. The hurt and heartbreak she'd lived with for
far too long came through in every tear that soaked the
front of Pike's shirt when he took her in a crushing hold.

"I never stopped Isak. Loving you-I never stopped.
You have to know that too."

"Prove it."

His expression was closed when she pulled back to
look at him.

He shrugged. "Prove it. Come back to me. Christ
Bella," he muttered when she bit her lip as though she were
debating. "How many ways do I have to tell you that this
shit doesn't matter to me? What matters is I need you, love
you...I don't care too much for the guy I am without you."

"I *do* love you." She said.

"Prove it, then." His sleek brows rose in challenge. "Come back to me."

She smiled. "That's the only way I can prove it?"

"Well…" it was his turn to debate. "There're many ways, but that one is at the top of my list."

"Hmm…" Belle pretended to ponder over her answer. "There's only one way I could see that happening, then."

"Really?" he was nudging her ear with his nose. "What way is that?"

"As your wife," Belle bit down on her lip again that time fixing him with a purely innocent look.

"Damn right." He confirmed with a chuckle that mingled with hers before silencing with their kiss.

***

Belle's hospital room was filled with soft laughter late the following afternoon. She was watching an Italian game show on the small TV that hung from the ceiling. She couldn't make out the Italian, but the humor came through without the need for translation.

The room door opened a tad and Belle looked over expecting to see Pike. She saw her mother instead.

Carmen remained in the doorway, training her gaze toward the floor when Belle looked over at her. "Isak told me you were sleeping." She shifted her weight from one foot to the other. "I can go if I'm disturbing-"

"Mama?"

A Lover's Shame

Carmen looked up; seeing Belle's extended hand, she ran to grab hold. "Isak said you know," she kissed Belle's palms, "he said you've known...please don't hate me. My sweet girl...anything I've gone through would be like nothing compared to what I'd suffer if you hate me now."

"Mama," Belle pulled Carmen to sit on the edge of the bed," I could never hate you but I have to wonder... why *you* don't hate *me*."

"Baby..." Bewilderment shadowed Carmen's honey toned features. "Hate *you*?" She looked as though the possibility of that were inconceivable.

"Why did you keep me Mama? You could've... gotten rid of me and had a fantastic life."

"I *have* a fantastic life." Fire kindled in Carmen's eyes then.

Belle averted her gaze. "But every day- *every day* I must've reminded you. What he did...why did you keep me Mama? No one would've blamed you for not keeping a child you didn't want-who was forced on you."

"Shh..." Carmen bowed her head for a time. "I didn't want what happened but I wanted *you*. With every part of me, I wanted you."

"But why?"

Carmen brushed the glossy locks across Belle's shoulder and smiled. "Part of it was curiosity. I wanted to know what your eyes would look like, what your voice would sound like." She tapped a finger to Belle's mouth.

"I wanted to know how your skin would feel next to mine." She rubbed her cheek next to Belle's before they embraced tightly. "I wanted to know what you'd feel like when I held you."

"The other reason," she said once she'd pulled back, "it may've had to do with the fact that you might not be his at all."

"What?" Belle pushed up higher against the pillows.

"I was in love- so in love… it was a long time ago. I was with him just before… it happened."

"Mama…" Belle leaned back next to the pillows and thought. "Why didn't you ever try to find out for sure?"

Carmen focused on tracing the crease in her pin-striped trousers. "I was too afraid to *know* for sure. The possibility that you could've been Marc's was easier to live with than the *reality* of you being his- stupid I know."

Belle shook her head. "You gave up so much. You could've been with the man you loved and happy."

A coy smile touched Carmen's lips and she looked up. "Life's a funny thing. Things you believe are lost forever have a way of coming back around. Like you and Isak." The lightness of her expression fell into shadow. "You overheard me that day. Isak left you at the house and you overheard me and Briselle, didn't you?" She closed her eyes, hissing a curse when Belle nodded.

"I'll never be able to make up for that."

Belle reached over and pulled Carmen's hands into hers. "Do you think we can stop trying to make up for things we can't change and try moving past them?"

A Lover's Shame

The brightness returned to Carmen's eyes then. "I can do that," she nodded and scooted closer, "I can do anything as long as I have you."

"You'll always have me, Mama."

Carmen's laughter mingled with happy tears while she held her daughter close.

***

That evening when Sabella woke from her nap, it took her some time to realize she wasn't alone. In fact, she stared in the direction of the man seated across her hospital room for some time. He didn't move or speak a word. Belle could just make out his image amidst the powerful stream of moonlight fighting past the blinds on the windows.

When he stood, she reached over quickly and switched on the lamp at her bedside. Whatever unease she'd been feeling over his unexpected movement, diminished when she looked into his face. He was older yet; despite the silky close cut silver hair, Belle guessed it'd be difficult to pinpoint his age. That probably had as much to do with his handsome dark face as with the tall lean build that could rival one of a man half his age.

"Are you a doctor?" She already knew the answer but figured it'd be up to her to open the floor for conversation. He smiled and she noticed his eyes were an uncommon shade of brown. They crinkled invitingly at the corners.

"No Love," he cleared his throat and moved closer to claim the chair nearest her bed. "No, I...I was a friend to your mother. Many years ago she saved me...from myself.

It seems she's returned to my life after all this time to save me yet again."

Belle sat up slowly. "Who are you?"

Jasper Stone leaned forward bracing elbows to knees and watching his fingers form a bridge. "If not for a very unfortunate occurrence, I would have been your mother's husband and a father to a beautiful girl." He smiled again, but that time there was something more awe-filled in the warm pools of his brown eyes.

"Life is strange," he smirked. "You see, I've never been a husband but it seems I may have been a father for over thirty years."

"Who are you?" Her voice caught.

Jasper placed his hand palm-up on the bed. "To answer that question, beauty, I'll need your consent."

A Lover's Shame

SEVENTEEN

The following days dragged on endlessly. Belle thought she'd go stir crazy if the doctors didn't release her soon. Her need to be admitted in the first place had been something of a blessing. Dr. Bottazzi had informed her that she'd gone through some form of withdrawal. She hadn't been taking the prescription properly in the first place. Once Pike had come back into the picture and all the unrest that had followed his return, her thoughts were miles away from following the regiment for the medication.

Thankfully, the monotony of those hospital days was made more bearable by Pike. He was by her side on most days until she fell asleep at night. On one particular afternoon, she woke to the dual treat of finding both her fiancé and her mother there.

Carmen was reading while Pike handled a phone call as the TV droned softly in the background. Still drowsy, Belle let her lashes drift down over her eyes again. She felt cared for, loved and very secure.

Even still, she couldn't keep her thoughts off the man who'd visited her almost a week earlier. He'd left her with his name, took a sample of her DNA and a vial of her blood. She hadn't seen him since.

Perhaps he'd been part of a dream, she thought. Perhaps it was a dream where Marcus Ramsey was her uncle and nothing more. A dream where her mother was living a full happy life with the man she loved. A dream where Belle imagined she was doing the same.

"Isn't there something you can do to make them let me out of here *today*?" Belle decided she'd played the role of the well-mannered patient for long enough.

Pike grinned while settling his tall athletic frame near the head of the bed. "What do you suggest I do?" He tugged at the lacy collar of her gown and raised his brows when she looked back at him. "More importantly, what do I get for my trouble?"

Belle pretended to mull over the question for a few seconds. Then, she snapped her fingers. "I could marry you."

"Wow," Pike made a phony display of surprise. "You'd actually marry a guy like me?"

Belle giggled when she nodded.

"Well if that's the case…" He dug around in the front pocket of his black denim shirt. "You should have a ring at least."

All teasing was set aside when Belle set sight on the ring glittering like a beam of pure illumination.

"Isak…"

"I know it's bigger than the first one I gave you." His darkly gorgeous features softened when he faked a show of unease. "Hope you don't mind. I've got more money now. Besides," he pushed the band onto her finger, "A new ring for a new time."

"An eternity," Belle wasn't looking at the ring but into his eyes.

"And then some," Pike added and tugged her into a sweet kiss which was interrupted by a knock to the door.

Carmen stuck her head inside the room. "Sorry for interrupting. There's someone I want you both to meet."

Belle didn't pretend not to recognize Jasper Stone when he stepped into the room behind her mother.

"It's nice to see you again." She told him. "I was afraid I was dreaming when I met you."

Jasper moved close and brushed his fingers across her cheek. "So was I, Love." He nodded towards Pike and extended his hand. "Jasper Stone," he said.

"Well now I'm at a complete loss." Carmen pushed her hand into a side pocket on her pleated skirt. "I came here to introduce you, but I see that's not necessary."

"I'm happy to see things back on track between you and Sabella." Jasper still addressed Pike. "I hope that doesn't mean we can't stay in touch. After all," he came to kiss Belle's forehead. "My little girl and I have lost a lot of time. I'm afraid I'm gonna need a bit of it now."

Belle's mouth fell open but it was Carmen who shrieked Jasper's name. Pike sat bewildered while Belle reached out to take the man's hand.

"I had the tests run twice." Jasper sat at the foot of the bed. "You're free to run them again if further re-confirmation is needed." He nodded toward Pike.

Carmen moved to Jasper's side. "How could you have run tests with Marc-" she cut herself off.

Belle nodded toward Jasper and then tugged her mother's hand. "I know what happened to him Mama."

"I ran the first tests using mine and Sabella's DNA. It was a match but I ran Marc's just to rule him out."

"How is that possible if the man's dead?" Pike had regained his verbal faculties. "Burned alive, according to my cousin," he slanted Belle a sly wink when she looked at him across her shoulder.

A Lover's Shame

Jasper shrugged. "I had some of my associates pay the fool a visit to collect the necessary samples. He didn't protest much."

Overwhelmed then, Carmen dropped into the nearest chair. "She's yours?"

Jasper moved from the bed and pulled Carmen into his arms. "She's mine. She's mine, Carm."

"Jasper..." her eyes followed the path her hands smoothed across his chest, "Jasper I-"

"Hey?" He shook his head. "We're done with regrets and apologies, right?" He kissed her temple.

Pike reached for Belle's hand and gave it a squeeze.

"I think it's time for celebrating." Jasper said and turned to face his daughter and her fiancé.

"I agree," Belle snuggled into Pike as a hint of seriousness crept into her expressive brown eyes. "I hope we can also agree to keep this between the four of us- and aunt Bri of course." She smiled toward Carmen.

"The family's been through too much. Knowing this would be *too* much." Belle waited and then sighed her relief when everyone nodded their consent.

"Well then," Pike said once the silence had carried long enough, "if everybody's in the mood to celebrate, I know of a wedding that'll be taking place soon."

Belle nodded eagerly then cupped Pike's face and planted a hard kiss to his mouth.

"Very soon," she corrected.

***

Las Vegas, Nevada~

"It's pronounced the same as Issac with two Ss and one C. Only it's got one S and a K. Screw this up and screw up your paycheck. Dumpy jackass," Sabra Ramsey muttered as she stormed away from the man who'd been hired to announce the wedding party.

On her way through the crowded reception hall of her second tower, Sabra was pulled in one direction after another. She'd returned every handshake and smiled over every compliment. Only when she was pulled aside by her aunt, did she allow any frustration to show.

"Good job, lil girl." Catrina Ramsey tugged her niece into a loose hug and kissed her cheek. "Lovely event, absolutely lovely."

"Thanks Aunt Cat," Sabra held onto Catrina's hand slung over her shoulder. "That means a lot coming from my catering party planning aunt especially since they only gave me a few weeks to plan this thing."

"Oh hush and stop acting put out," Catrina bumped Sabra's hip with hers. "You know you would've been pissed if they hadn't asked you to give the reception."

"Hmph. No… I'll be pissed if I ever have to throw them another one. People that much in love shouldn't even know how to *spell* the word divorce, let alone go through with one." Sabra tossed her hair across her shoulder in a pretend huff.

Catrina nodded toward the *people* in question. "I think they understand that now."

A Lover's Shame

Sabra smiled and dropped her arm across Catrina's shoulder. "Yeah Aunt Cat, I think you're right."

Much of the wedding party had left the head table to mingle and dance leaving the newlyweds to their own devices.

"When can we get the hell out of here?" Pike spoke softly against his wife's ear.

"Don't even try it." Belle giggled and tugged at his white tuxedo sleeve. "It was *your* idea to have this big wedding."

"Correction Bella, the *wedding* was small. I got no idea how the reception turned into such an *event*."

"Ah. I can answer that in one word- Sabra."

Pike winced and ran his finger around the inside of his collar. "She'd have killed me if we'd put it together without her."

"Mmm," Belle nodded against his shoulder. "She'd have definitely killed *you*- slow and easy."

The couple was still laughing when a beefy olive skinned man walked up to the table.

"Congratulations, kid."

"Mr. Nandi." Pike stood and greeted the man with a hearty shake and double cheek kiss. "Thanks for coming."

"Ah!" the heavy set man gave a flip wave yet smiled broadly.

"Bella," Pike reached out to squeeze her hand, "you may not remember but this is Fredrico Nandi- CFO of Tesano-Nandi. He and my grandfather started the textile manufacturing end of the company when they were barely in their twenties. It's still the cornerstone of Tesano Industries."

"Stop boy!" Fredrico Nandi dropped a loud clap to Pike's shoulder. "You give me too much credit! It was Liam with all that vision of his. Left up to me, we'd still be sellin' fabric." He looked down at Belle, took her hand and kissed it.

"You are as mesmerizing as you were the first time this kid took you for his bride." Fredrico kissed the back of her other hand. "Be happy." He straightened then, reached into his tailored suit coat and withdrew a thick envelope which he pressed into Pike's hand.

"She's too beautiful to let go twice in a lifetime. See that you don't."

Pike looked down at Belle and shook his head. "Never again," He vowed, and then hugged and kissed Nandi a second time. When the man strolled away, Pike pushed the envelope into the nearby satchel that bulged with scores of envelopes carrying money which totaled in the hundreds of thousands of dollars.

Belle eyed the white leather bag with a raised brow. "That'll come in handy." She teased.

Pike's face flushed beneath its bronzed-tone as he blushed in embarrassment. "It's tradition."

"I remember." She said.

"I don't know why they bother." He propped his fist to his chin and studied the bag warily. "They know I won't keep it- add more money to the pot of my granddad's foundation or some other worthy cause." He shrugged.

Belle brushed her thumb across the gold band adorning his finger. "That sounds like a good idea. I think your little boy or little girl sounds like a worthy cause."

Pike's ebony stare was on the satchel. "Yeah it-" His head whipped around and his eyes fell to her waist. "Belle..." his already soft voice sounded even fainter.

"Doctor Bottazzi told me before we left Italy." She fingered one of the tendrils that dangled outside the chignon she wore. "He waited until he thought I was strong enough to hear it. I wanted to surprise you." She took a breath and offered a dazzling smile. "Looks like we're about to contribute more than money to the family, huh?"

Pike bowed his head to her stomach. For almost a full minute, he whispered something reverent yet too soft to clearly make out.

"Are you okay with this?" she asked when he looked up at her. "We didn't have time to discuss-Mmm..."

He was kissing her deeply and without a care for who might witness such a passionate display. Belle reciprocated without hesitation. Her nails scraped his now clean-shaved face and she moaned unabashed as her tongue wrestled with his. She laughed. Glee and euphoria didn't seem to be apt descriptions to relay the extent of her happiness but they were the best she could come up with at the time.

A throat cleared overhead, silenced and then cleared again to be followed by soft laughter when the couple finally broke their kiss. Belle's laughter resumed as well when she looked up and saw the very tall, very dark and very attractive man leaning against the table. Pike smirked and stood to extend a hand toward his brother.

"So you decided to make this one?" Pike teased.

Smoak Tesano's gaze was just as dark and bottomless as his older brother's. "I'm guessing this'll be the *last* one."

"Damn straight," Pike said while he and Smoak hugged across the table.

Belle was next to tug her brother-in-law close. "I'm so glad you're here." She whispered once he'd swung her up high and kissed her mouth. "It's good to see you." She said once they'd embraced for many moments.

"*You're* the one it's good to see." Smoak countered, his gaze crinkling as it appraised her.

"I guess you'll be around for a while?" Belle asked, though it was clear she already knew the answer.

Smoak offered a one-shoulder shrug. "For better or worse, right?"

Belle pressed her lips together and appeared to be debating her next statement. She glanced quickly toward Pike and then gave Smoak a resolute smile. "She'll kill me for telling you this, but she's not as tough and flip as she likes to come across. So just um…"

"Hey?" Smoak cupped Belle's cheek and waited for her to look up at him. "I'm not here to hurt her. I have no intentions of doing that. Please believe me?"

A Lover's Shame

Belle squeezed his hand and nodded. "I'll just give you guys some privacy." She tugged the handkerchief peeking from Smoak's tuxedo jacket, smiled at her husband and then strolled off into the crowd.

"I'll have you committed if you let her leave you again." Smoak told his brother, his dark eyes following Belle until she'd disappeared into the sea of bodies.

"That won't ever happen, but you've got my consent at any rate." Pike kept his stare focused on the general direction his wife had taken. "Sabra may not be as tough as she likes to pretend, but I still say you're risking your life by showin' your face here." He set his hands into his trouser pockets and waited.

Smoak grinned while bowing his head. "This I know." He muttered.

"So what's up?" Pike tilted his head for a better view of his brother's face. "You've taken over an entire floor of the place? You tryin' to fuck with her head or are you really concerned?"

"I'm past concerned." Smoak studied his palm before clenching a fist and looking over at his brother.

"Should we all be doing what you are? Camping out at our women's places of business?"

"I don't want to be responsible for a panic." Smoak was back to studying his hand, working a thumb into the center of his palm. "I'll know better how to answer that once I talk to Dad."

As if he were waiting on his cue, Roman was next to arrive at the long table. He supplied hearty claps to his sons' backs and pulled them into double hugs and cheek kisses.

"I need to see you both. Tenth floor conference room in an hour."

Suspicious, the younger men shared glances.

"Pop-"

"An hour, alright?" Roman lifted a hand to silence Pike. "Besides," he said when Belle returned to the table, "I've got a beauty to take for a twirl." He said and whisked the laughing bride to the dance floor.

"What do you think?"

Smoak was shaking his head. "Nothin' good."

Pike took a seat along the edge of the table. "Have you seen her yet?"

"Yeah," the pain in Smoak's clear deep voice matched what dwelled in his midnight eyes. "I um- she doesn't know I'm here though."

It was Pike's turn to shake his head then. "So how long will you stick to this vow not to touch her? It's gotta be hell on you every time you see her."

The hard angles of Smoak's darkly devastating face seemed to take on a more rigid set. "You have no idea," he confessed.

Pike had a fine idea of what his brother was going through and made a silent vow to ease up on the questioning. He squeezed Smoak's shoulder. "Don't waste the time you've got, alright? You do what's necessary to get her back."

***

A Lover's Shame

"I can't believe you let this fool get you pregnant." SyBilla Ramsey rolled her eyes in pretend outrage while watching her cousin and his wife cuddle across the table they shared.

"Pray for me." Tykira begged, giggling while Quaysar massaged her shoulders beneath the satin straps of her lilac dress.

Bill folded her arms over the front of the asymmetrical mocha jacket she sported. "Honey, I think you're gonna need more than prayer."

Quay flashed his cousin a look of pretend hurt. "That's cold, Bill."

The group fell into laughter and then a three-way hug that ended when Quay pulled back to glare at the man who had approached the table.

"Tesano." Quay greeted in a tone that sounded nothing close to welcoming.

Caiphus Tesano wore a polite expression in spite of the chilly acknowledgement. "Congratulations on the baby, you two."

Ty wore the only smile of anyone at the table. "Thanks so much, Caiphus." She said.

Nodding, Caiphus' brilliant teal stare slid toward SyBilla. "Could I have a minute, Bee?"

"Hmph," Quay gestured, and then grunted in pain when Ty planted an elbow into his ribs.

Bill gave no response but stood and left the table silently offering her consent.

"No glasses?" She noted when they were cornered off in a small alcove.

Caiphus trailed his finger along a sleek brow. "Laser surgery. I only need glasses when I read."

"I'm impressed." Bill leaned back on six inch spiked heels and regarded him as if she were anything but. "I would've thought you too much of a coward to go through with something like that. I would've at least thought you too vain to risk a scar."

Caiphus chuckled, genuine humor filling the gesture. "Bee, Bee always thinking the worst of me." He leaned against the wall and brought his head close to hers. "I thought I'd hear from you before now."

"Surprised, were you?" She tried to mimic his calm by opting for a leaning stance as well and hoped he couldn't hear her heart trying to beat out of her chest. "Lamont's the gullible one, not me." She referred to her boss. "I figured that file he showed me was a sham."

"Sham?" His chuckle held more disbelief than humor. "That's my career, I'll have you know."

"Right," Bill hid her hands in the deep pockets of her satin pants. "All those outrageous, dangerous ops you and your supposed crew have run over the last nine years, all yours?"

"I turned from my wayward ways when you left me."

"Hmph. No, all you did was con the government into believing you walk on water when it comes to taking down various crime syndicates. Funny how your family isn't among the casualties."

Caiphus had reached out to toy with a short curly tendril of SyBilla's hair. "Would you like for me to prove it, Bee?"

She braced off the wall and trusted herself to take a step closer to tug the open collar of the crisp shirt beneath the jacket of his tux. "Well you see that'd be impossible since I take everything you say- to me, that is- as a lie. Goodbye Caiphus." The hand pat she laid against his cheek had all the earmarks of a slap.

"What the hell...?" Sabra's long stare narrowed to twin slits when she spotted two familiar faces. The estate lawyers had already spotted her so she simply waited for their approach.

"Ms. Ramsey. Quite the gathering." Russell Byrd's voice was breathy with excitement as he looked around the crowded reception hall.

Sabra wasn't flattered. "Quite. What are you two doing here?"

Bradley Carroll's excitement matched his partner's. "Well it's that time again, you know?"

Sabra folded her arms over a sparkling crop vest and didn't attempt to mask her agitation. "So what are you guys doing *here* and not in Phoenix?"

The law partners passed glances between one another.

"Why Mr. Tesano asked that we all meet here in Las Vegas to sign the papers this year."

"He said he'd inform you."

"Well he didn't." Sabra looked down her nose at Russell Byrd. "When did the three of you discuss this?"

"Why last year when we met to sign the papers," Bradley Carroll shared.

"Is that the last time you saw him?"

"Well-" Bradley's small green eyes sparkled with knowing. "It *was*."

Sabra didn't waste time trying to prepare herself. She turned quickly, surprised that she was able to remain on her feet with Smoak Tesano a mere five feet in front of her.

He closed what remained of that brief distance and came to graze the back of his hand along her bare arm riddled with gooseflesh.

"Will this be a problem for us?" He asked.

Imani planted another set of double kisses to Belle's cheeks. They'd been talking, reminiscing and simply enjoying one another's company for the better part of ten minutes.

"I can only pray that the rest of my sons will get it together and keep it together the way you and Isak have fought to."

Belle studied the bold embroidery along the cuff of the floor length royal blue and gold jacket matching

A Lover's Shame

Imani's dress. "Guess they have to choose their women first."

"Oh they all did that long ago." Imani gave a graceful wave of one hand. "They just haven't quite figured out how to claim them." Her dark, beautiful face brightened with a smile. "Well…one has." She said as Pike approached with Carmen on his arm.

Imani opened her arms to Carmen, who bent to take part in a tight embrace.

"Looks like we're in-laws again!" Imani cried.

Carmen laughed. "I hope you don't mind!"

Imani pulled back to look at Carmen but kept her hands tight on her arms. "Never have and never will." She said, laughing as they hugged again.

Carmen straightened and extended a hand to Sabella. "Baby could we talk for a minute?"

Pike took the spot next to Imani once Belle had excused herself to speak with Carmen. He pulled his mother close, kissed her mouth and rested his head on her shoulder.

After a moment, Imani eased back to search his eyes with hers. "There's my sweet guy," she whispered, "He was hidden away under so much darkness."

Like Belle had done earlier, Pike studied the elaborate stitching along Imani's traditional attire. "I don't want to lose it Ma- the darkness… I um…" Idly, he traced the back of her hand. "I may need to draw on certain… strengths that darker guy had before it's all over."

Imani's expression mirrored understanding. "We all need a bit of darkness inside us- helps us to recognize the good more easily. Keeps us balanced," she squeezed his face. "As long as you don't draw on too much. Never too much."

Mother and son hugged again. Imani's hold that time was noticeably tighter. When Pike pulled back, his gaze was questioning.

"Can I take you back to your room?" He asked, believing she was exhausting herself.

Imani was shaking her head. "Not until I see you dance with your wife."

"But you're alright?" Pike tilted his head to study her intently.

Imani gave an honest, happy laugh. "My love, I swear I've never felt better!"

"Oh Mama, I understand. I know how busy he is."

"Things came up so unexpectedly. It was more than a little shocking when I realized what a busy man your father is. Lord…" Carmen laughed as her light eyes suddenly misted with tears. "I'm sorry I-I prayed for him to be your father, lived my life believing he was and to know now for sure it's still a lot to take in." Nervously, she ran her hands along the sides of her elegant peach A-lined dress.

"Shh…" Belle leaned close to squeeze her mother for long moments.

A Lover's Shame

"Anyway," Carmen patted Belle's waist and stepped back. "He wants you two to enjoy this dream honeymoon as his present. Everything's arranged on yours and Isak's timetable. You'll find all the information in your suite."

Belle shook her head, regretting Jasper wasn't there for her to hug and thank in person. "He didn't need to do all of that. I'd be happy with Isak anywhere." Tears got the better of her then too. "God Mama, do we really deserve to be this happy?"

"I don't know!" Carmen laughed. "But I'm not about to complain!"

Laughter and hugs resumed.

***

"Ladies and Gentlemen may I have your attention please! I'd like for you to join me in bestowing our wishes for an eternity of love and prosperity to our newlyweds Isak and Sabella Tesano!"

Thunderous applause and cheers roared through the massive crowd. The announcer let the applause go for little over a minute before raising his hands for silence.

"Mr. Tesano would you care to dance with your wife?"

A silence covered the hall then. Pike stood and offered his hand to Belle. She obliged and grasped the elegant folds of the crème gown that billowed about and gave her the look of a fairy princess.

The newlyweds took to the floor just as the stirrings of Roberta Flack's *"The First Time Ever I Saw Your Face"* drifted into the air. The ballad was the epitome of love and devotion. It added yet another special layer to a beautiful moment.

Belle smoothed her hand down the side of Pike's face as the opening lyrics of the ballad stirred. He pressed his forehead to hers and closed his eyes to savor the satiny feel of her skin as his thumb roamed the curve of her cheek and jaw.

The song combined with the almost tangible emotion surrounding the two. The crowd's attention was completely riveted upon them. As far as Pike and Belle were concerned, they were the only two who existed in the room.

"I love you very much." He said, only loud enough for her to hear.

"You're everything to me." She spoke the words in a manner just as soft and linked her arms about her husband's neck while his eased about her waist.

Locked in the embrace, they swayed as the sweet ballad mirrored what echoed in their hearts.

Dear Reader,

I usually wait until my final draft is typed and ready to be submitted before writing this letter. I decided to write this letter upon finishing the first draft. I was just that moved to do so. There were so many elements I wanted to bring to Pike's and Belle's story that I really wasn't sure that it was possible. I was so certain that something would be lost in the translation between what was filling my heart about the couple and the storyline and what would eventually come through on paper.

This is the story that sets the stage for the final act in what has been a truly rewarding experience. The Ramseys have challenged me, fulfilled me, and stunned me by where they've demanded I take them. I have felt such satisfaction while weaving this tale. Now, with the introduction of the Tesanos and their part in the saga, that fulfillment is being taken to another level.

Many of you have asked if I know how the whole thing ends and I've said yes. This is most certainly true however the route to that ending will not be a straight line. I hope you're prepared for where this story will take you. I know that I'm prepared to write it. Please know that your support is such a huge factor in my ability to do what I do. Thanks for joining me on this journey.

Love and Blessings,
AlTonya
altonya@lovealtonya.com
www.lovealtonya.com

ALTONYA'S TITLE LIST

Remember Love
Guarded Love
Finding Love Again
Love Scheme
Wild Ravens (Historical)
In The Midst of Passion
A Lover's Dream (Ramsey I)
A Lover's Pretense (Ramsey II)
Pride and Consequence
A Lover's Mask (Ramsey III)
A Lover's Regret (Ramsey IV)
A Lover's Worth (Ramsey V)
Soul's Desire (Ebook/Short Story)
Through It All (Ebook/Novella)
Rival's Desire
Hudson's Crossing
Passion's Furies (Historical)
A Lover's Beauty (Ramsey VI)
A Lover's Soul (Ramsey VII)
Lover's Allure (Ramsey Romance Novella)
A Ramsey Wedding (Novella)
Book of Scandal- The Ramsey Elders
Another Love
Expectation of Beauty (YA Romance)
Truth In Sensuality (Erotica)
Ruler of Perfection (Erotica)
The Doctor's Private Visit
As Good As The First Time
Every Chance I Get

FIND ALTONYA ON THE WEB

www.lovealtonya.com
www.facebook.com
www.shelfari.com/novelgurl
www.goodreads.com

An AlTonya Exclusive